WICKED DARKNESS

VICTORIA ZAK

VICTORIA ZAK ROMANCE

Copyright

Wicked Darkness - Victoria Zak
Copyright 2018 by Victoria Zak

Cover Design: JAB Designs

Editing: Violetta Rand

❀ Created with Vellum

CONTENTS

Sign up for Victoria Zak's newsletter at her website to receive a free ebook copy of her Guardians of Scotland novella
Highland Destiny

You'll also find additional special offers, bonus content and info on new releases.

www.victoriazakromance.com
victoria@victoriazakromance.com

1

EVIL LINGERED IN THE AIR. And for someone like Leana, who had fallen from grace so long ago, it felt perfect. Masked by her black cloak, she slipped inside the familiar tavern she'd been visiting for over a month, chose her usual seat in the back of the room, and wondered where a certain woman had gotten to. Leana's latest target, a lass that never deviated from her daily routine.

"Wine?" A voice asked a nearby patron.

Leana closed her eyes and breathed in the intoxicating fragrance of heather and bog myrtle. The killer inside her resurfaced, dominating her every thought. Her gums ached as she recalled how easily her fangs could rip into flesh. Especially the soft skin on a delicate neck. *Ye must be patient, Leana,* her darker side warned. She found it difficult to resist her natural cravings, that constant temptation to revert back to her lower self, the creature that preyed upon the weak.

Leana wasn't ashamed of who or what she was—she wore it proud like a crown upon her head. She gripped the edge of the table, her sharp black nails splintering the wood. She hadn't spent the last month studying Davina's every move just to surrender to her hunger and ruin everything she'd planned so carefully. If she'd intended for the lass to be a simple meal, she would have killed her the first day. Nay, this time Leana had a purpose.

She'd watched Davina and knew her every move as if it were her own. With her eyes closed, Leana heard the wine splashing into the tankard at the next table, even smelled her hair. Her flirtatious laughter made Leana smile. *Aye, the lass was perfect.*

Leana opened her eyes to find Davina standing next to her. The lass didn't look well. Her eyes were swollen and red and her skin much paler than the day before.

"Mistress." Davina coughed into a cloth. The stench of blood awakened the *Baobhan sith's* hunger inside Leana.

"Please, sit," Leana motioned to the chair across the table. "Ye need rest."

"I can no'." The lass looked around the tavern. "I must get back to work."

Leana pulled back her hood and stared into the lass's eyes. "Ye want to sit with me, Davina." With a single look, Leana could influence the mind of a human, bend Davina to her will.

Confusion creased Davina's face. "How do ye know my name?"

"There's no one here but ye and I."

Davina sat down.

Luck was on Leana's side. The stronger willed the victim, the harder it was to manipulate their mind. But Davina was different—she was ill. Her mind was weak. "Ye are no' well, lass."

"How do ye know?"

"I can smell heather and bog myrtle on yer breath.

Everyone knows that's a remedy for fever. I know what ails ye."

"How? Can ye see the demon?"

Demon? That was ridiculous. It was clear the lass was suffering from a weak heart.

"The priest said I should ask God for forgiveness for my sins. God is punishing me, but for what, I dinnae know."

Leana held the lass's hand. "There's no' demon in ye. Ye have a failing heart."

Leana sat back, watching Davina. Compassion broke through her savagery, planting the tiniest seed of sympathy for the lass. She could heal Davina. *"Keep yer promise to yer sisters. Dinnae take an innocent life,"* her conscious warned.

But Davina had something Leana wanted—her life.

The unfortunate lass matched Leana in every way with her long red hair, slender body, and pale skin. She had no family, so no one would notice if she disappeared and Leana took over her body.

Faking her own death was the only way for Leana to trick the fae queen into believing she had died. The queen wanted her, for it was Leana who had called upon the fae for help. She'd made the blood oath that had changed her sisters' lives.

With Leana gone, her sisters, Adaira and Masie, would stop searching for her and live productive lives. It was the only way to protect them. In the past Leana had always tried to do the right thing, but always ended up hurting someone she loved. Not this time.

Leana exhaled. This wasn't the time for her conscious to take a righteous stance.

"Lass." Leana leaned forward. "I can take yer pain away. All ye have to do is ask." If Davina wanted to end her suffering, it wouldn't feel like Leana had taken an innocent life. The fae queen had taught her so well.

"I dinnae understand," Davina said. "The priest said I would die. How can ye heal me?"

"Lass, I never said I would heal ye. All I said was I can take the pain away. No more coughing up blood, no more weakness, no more pain." Leana looked around the tavern. "Ye would no' have to work here anymore. Dinnae ye grow tired of men putting their hands all over ye?"

"Aye." Davina coughed.

"Dinnae ye want to leave all this loneliness behind?"

"Aye."

"I can give ye what ye seek."

"Death?"

"All ye have to do is ask."

Davina lowered her head. "I'm in so much pain."

"I know, lass." Leana squeezed her hand. Sorrow welled in Davina's eyes causing Leana's cold heart to crack with sympathy.

"I've wasted my life. I was too scared to live outside these four walls." Davina looked around the Tavern. "My dreams of marrying a loving man never came true. I should have conquered life and taken what I wanted. Instead, I stayed here with the bottom of the barrel eejits." Davina sobbed into her hands.

Leana caught a tear from Davina's cheek. The loneliness, regret, and agony that plagued the lass filled Leana with immeasurable hunger. If she wasn't careful, her inner beast would be unleashed. "Ask me," Leana commanded.

Davina slowly looked up from the floor. She stared into Leana's eyes, completely bewitched.

"Good, lass," Leana whispered. "Ye want to ask me something, aye?"

Davina nodded. "Take me to the void. Kill me."

Leana's lips curled into a wicked grin. The plan was working beautifully. Manipulating Davina's mind was too easy. "Ye will obey every word I say."

Davina nodded.

"Ye can no' breathe."

The lass clutched her chest and gasped for air.

"Ye need fresh air. Go outside and wait for me."

"Aye." Davina quickly stood.

"Dinnae talk to anyone. Go unseen," Leana said.

The lass made her way out of the tavern.

Relieved, Leana exhaled. No matter how many times she'd controlled a human's mind, it still made her nervous. The mind was powerful and unpredictable. If one thing went wrong, an unexpected scream or a bold accusation against her, Leana could be accused of witchery and burned at the stake. Nay, she wasn't going to become kindling for a bonfire.

Leana pulled her hood over her head and walked outside. Her new life awaited.

The cold, night air bit into Leana's skin as she followed Davina's footprints into the glen behind the tavern. Her blood pumped wildly through her veins with the need to kill. Aye, Davina waited just beyond the trees. Leana licked her lips as everything turned red. Her fangs extended, and animal-like power consumed her. Shite, the beast was there. Like lightening, she stalked through the glen—ready to attack, ready to kill, ready to change her own life.

She found her prey standing beside the shallow grave she'd dug earlier.

"How long have ye been planning me death?" Davina asked.

The lass's mind was under Leana's control, so why was

she asking questions? Had she missed something about Davina? "Who are ye?"

"Ye should know. Ye've been stalking me."

What was happening? Had Leana been tricked? Was the queen behind this? Perhaps she should go before something happened...

"Dinnae leave," Davina said. "I want to die. And it's my choice. But why me? Why am I chosen?"

Leana didn't know what to say, nor was she obligated to explain herself. "The real question here is why I can no' compel yer mind." Leana studied Davina. "What are ye?"

"What do ye mean? I'm an orphan. 'Tis all I know."

"But ye know who—" Leana paused. Mayhap the lass didn't know that a blood drinker was standing in front of her.

"Know what?"

"The truth is, I want yer life and I can no' have it if ye're still alive."

"Why would ye want to be me? I'm nothing."

"Davina, yer life matters to me."

"Why? Who are ye running from?"

Maiden, Mother, Crone. "It does no' matter why I chose ye or who I'm running from." *Because ye'll be dead.* "Ye'll no longer suffer. This life was no' yers to keep. Face death and cross into the void knowing yer new life begins in another time and place."

Davina braved looking at Leana.

The first time Leana had seen Davina, her eyes were filled with sorrow. Perhaps that's what had attracted her to Davina, for Leana knew endless suffering, too. Something altogether different shined in the lass's eyes now. A flicker of something good. *Hope?*

"Who will send me to the void?" Davina asked.

"My name is Leana."

"Leana, promise ye'll live my life better than I have."

Once again, the lass had found a way to creep into Leana's heart. She paused, considering Davina's words carefully. If she healed the lass *Davina* could live her own life to its fullest. She'd find the man of her dreams, have many bairns.

Did Leana have the strength to ward off these weak human feelings and allow this woman to live?

Me sisters deserve to live. Davina must die.

"I promise."

The lass tipped her chin up. "I am ready."

Leana brushed Davina's long hair away from her face. A large vein ran down the side of her neck, her sweet life essence running through it. Leana's gums ached as her fangs descended.

Without a second thought, Leana's fangs stabbed through Davina's tender flesh. She sucked at the vein. Iron-tasting blood flowed across her tongue and down her throat, awaking her eternal thirst.

It didn't take long for Davina to wilt against Leana, too weak to stand on her own. Leana took another long taste, sealing Davina's fate. Her body went limp and her heart stopped beating.

Leana laid the body on the ground. She wiped the blood from her mouth with the back of her hand, catching her breath. She felt empty and numb. Though her plan had worked, she didn't feel any better. Why did she feel like there was something gripping at her heart and wouldn't let go? Remorse? Nay, she shook her head and quickly dismissed that wretched thought. She'd killed before, but somehow, this felt different.

Quickly, Leana switched dresses with the lass, then

placed Davina in the grave. Looking down at Davina, Leana shuddered. By switching clothes with the lass, Davina took on Leana's features. She picked up the shovel she'd left by the grave earlier and started to fill the grave with dirt. That's when she found her green, woolen cloak on the ground. She picked it up. Her Clan Keith white stag brooch was pinned to the cloak, and it reminded Leana of her sisters. Their mother had given them matching brooches. It was the only thing she had left from her family. She caressed the heirloom.

Everything must die with the lass.

Keeping anything that tied her to Leana Keith was a risk she wasn't willing to take. She threw the cloak and brooch inside the half-filled grave, then resumed shoveling. "The demons can no' harm ye anymore, Davina. Yer God will lay ye to rest." At least she hoped so for the lass's sake. "Goodbye, Leana Keith."

2

KENDRICK SAT at the head of the table drumming his fingers. His eldest daughter, Anna, still hadn't come home. To make matters worse, she had her five-year-old sister lie for her.

He refilled his ale cup, no stranger to drink. In fact, he'd become very fond of the taste and numbing effect when he overindulged. Though his wife had died five years ago giving birth to their youngest daughter, Allison, her loss felt fresh.

The door creaked open and Kendrick straightened, fighting the urge to leap across the table and run to his daughter to make sure she fared well.

"Da," his doe-eyed daughter said, shocked to see him awake at such a late hour.

He glared at her and folded his arms across his chest.

"I—I can explain."

"Ye have been with the MacTavish lad, aye?"

"Da—"

"It would be wise no' to lie to me, daughter," his tone hardened. "I'm in no mood."

Anna closed the door, avoiding his gaze.

Kendrick stood and made his way across the room. "I've told ye no' to see that lad anymore." He pulled a piece of hay from her tangled hair.

She pushed off the door, shouldering her way past him. "We're in love, da."

"Love!" Kendrick whipped around. The only thing that lad was after was his daughter's virtue. Love had nothing to with it. "He told ye that, and ye believed him?"

"Da!" Anna faced him. "I believe him. He wants to marry me."

Kendrick's heart sank to his stomach. Marriage? Nay, this was not a conversation he wanted to have with Anna. She was an innocent, too young to think of such things. "If ye will no' obey me rules, I'll send ye to the nunnery until I find a fit husband for ye."

"Ye wouldn't," Anna exclaimed.

"Aye, I would. I want better for you."

"Just because he's poor does no' make him any less of a man. MacTavish has worked yer land for years, and his parents have been loyal."

"Coin buys loyalty, Anna." Kendrick started up the stairs. As far as he was concerned, the discussion was over.

"Da, do no' walk away. I'm no' a little girl anymore."

Kendrick stopped half way up the stairs. "I know ye're a young lady. Why do ye think I'm trying to keep ye from making a mistake?"

Anna shrugged.

"If ye wish to make a good match, ye need to protect yer maidenhood."

"But I dinnae want to marry a man I do no' care about. I love MacTavish, and he loves me. He makes me happy, Da."

"Enough," Kendrick cut her off. "Ye're not to see that lad

again. In fact, ye are no' to leave this house until I say so, understood?"

"Nay," she refused. "Mum would never treat me this way." Anna stomped up the stairs.

"Anna," Kendrick called after her, but she continued to her room and slammed the door.

Kendrick's shoulders drooped in defeat. His daughter had a way of shaming him. Aye, her mother would have handled the situation better. Anna knew exactly how to cut him to the bone. His once loving daughter now hated him and blamed him for her mother's death. He'd not marry her to a servant.

He returned to the table in search of more drink, only to find the pitcher empty. He headed to the kitchen to get more ale. Spirits would warm his soul and make him forget, if only for a night.

The amber liquid warmed his body like a lover. "Adamina, I miss ye," he whispered as he stared into the flames in the hearth.

He needed his wife more than ever. Raising three children alone was hard. He didn't understand his daughters. Anna grew more and more rebellious. He'd caught Allie running around the kitchen wielding a wooden sword and cursing like a lad just yesterday. As a warrior, it warmed his heart to see his wee lass showing interest in fighting, but that kind of language from a five-year-old wasn't proper. Anna and Allie needed a mother.

His son Kit was the least of his problems. Every day he'd practice with his sword or plow the fields. His son waited to be called into service for the king. Though Kendrick knew devotion to the crown wasn't his reason for wanting to leave. The lad mourned his mother still. Would the lad find comfort in the bottle like Kendrick? The thought scared him.

Thank God he'd been blessed with hard-working tenants who helped keep his land going.

After a long, cold winter, the demand for barley and fresh beef from his herd of cattle must be satisfied in order to keep the local village fed.

Kendrick slumped back in his chair and sighed. Why couldn't he find the strength to take care of his family?

Without Adamina, the fight is gone.

Adamina had been the strength that kept their family together.

He closed his eyes and imagined her beautiful smile. "God's bones," he cursed. Living without her grew harder each day.

Kendrick took another drink, taking comfort that his wife still lived within his children. Anna had her smile, Kit had her witty humor, and Allie...many times he found himself unforgiving toward the child. He often blamed her for his wife's death, though he shouldn't. Their lives were unravelling, and Kendrick had no idea how to fix it.

3

COLD WATER RIPPED Kendrick from sleep. He shot up from the chair, dripping wet and angry. "What have ye done?" He glared at the bucket in Anna's hands.

Annoyed, Anna slammed the bucket on the table next to him. "Time for ye to wake up, Da."

All three of his children were staring at him.

"There's leftover porridge and bread on the table." Anna walked away with Allie.

"Da, I'll start a fire so ye dinnae catch yer death," Kit said as he began to throw wood into the hearth.

"Thank ye, son." Kendrick groaned, his head hurt.

"Finn will be here soon. Ye should try to eat something."

"Aye," Anna called from the kitchen. "And bathe. Ye reek of ale and vomit."

Kendrick sniffed the air and frowned. His tunic was soiled and the evidence of him getting sick from drinking too much was on the floor.

"Dinnae fash yerself, Da, I'll clean it up before Finn gets here," Kit said.

Kendrick staggered upstairs pretending there was

nothing wrong. But deep inside, he knew how bad it was for them to see him drunk, even if he pretended he didn't have a problem. Denial was easier than facing the truth.

Kendrick made it to his room, then washed and changed his clothes. He went back downstairs to eat.

Today, Kendrick had promised to help repair the old hay barn so the cattle currently staying in a pen behind Finn's house would have shelter. The beasts needed a place to stay warm.

Kendrick spooned porridge into his mouth. It was cold and didnae agree with his upset stomach. Mayhap an oat cake would be a better choice.

The knock at the door pounded through his head. Aye, he was in bad shape today.

Anna walked past him to answer the door. "Good morn, Finn."

"Good morn, Anna." He stepped inside.

"Da is breaking his fast." She motioned for Finn to sit at the table.

"Thank ye, lass." Finn took a seat across from Kendrick. "'Tis cold today."

"Aye. Have ye eaten?" Kendrick asked, offering him some porridge.

"It does no' matter if he hasn't eaten," Anna said. "I am done serving food."

"Och, Anna, where's yer manners?" Kendrick asked.

Anna ignored him as she bundled Allie in her fur-lined cloak. "I'm going to the MacGregor's to mend our clothes." Anna donned her cloak and picked up a basket with neatly folded clothes inside. "I can no' stand to be in this house any longer." She grabbed Allie's hand. "Come on."

Kendrick's heart melted as he watched his wee lass look back at him with a sad look.

"What did ye do to deserve that?" Finn asked.

"She snuck out last night to see MacTavish. She's angry because I caught her."

"Och, young love."

"Nay," Kendrick snapped. "'Tis no' love." He grabbed the last oat cake. "That lad wants to steal Anna's innocence, nothing more."

Finn shrugged. "She's coming of age, Kendrick."

Whose side was his best friend on? "Ye are the last person I should be having this conversation with."

"I agree," Finn said. "Ye need a wife."

Kendrick paused. *A wife?* What in the hell was Finn thinking? "I dinnae need another woman in this house. If ye haven't forgotten, I have two females here already. And that's enough."

"Have ye forgotten, I've known ye a long time. Yer house was in better hands when Adamina was alive."

"Ye know nothing about Adamina. I have everything under control."

Finn shook his head. "We've been through a lot together. I consider ye a brother. I dinnae want to see ye lose everything ye've worked so hard to have."

Kendrick finished the cake, then wiped his mouth. He leaned back in his chair, considering Finn's words. Both were born into unsettling times in Scotland where young boys were expected to become soldiers. They had saved each other's lives in numerous battles and seen a great deal of death. If it wasn't for Finn's friendship, Kendrick would have never made it through the hard times. Aye, Finn was his brother, and knew him better than anyone.

"Kendrick, ye're not the same man I used to know," Finn said. "Take a long look at yerself. Yer house is a mess. Yer children are unmanageable. Ye need a wife. Do it for yer children."

Kendrick shook his head, hating that Finn had a valid point. Hell, he was a solider. He'd led hundreds of men through battle, so why couldn't he win back his own house?

Because Adamina was gone.

Kendrick rubbed his chin. "Aye." Kendrick couldn't believe what he was about to say. "Ye're right."

"I have a plan."

Kendrick chuckled. Leave it to Finn to have thought it through for him.

"What?" Finn asked, his brows furrowed.

"Ye always have a plan, even off the battlefield."

"Aye, proper planning prevents poor performance."

"Och, ye have never performed proper in yer life. 'Tis why ye dinnae have a wife yerself." Kendrick walked to the door and grabbed his cloak.

Finn turned in his chair to face Kendrick. "Whether I perform proper or no' is beside the point. However, if ye must know, the lassies never complain."

"That's because they're too busy vomiting." They both laughed.

"Ye'll never let me forget that night, will ye," Finn asked as he stood and joined Kendrick by the front door.

"Nay, never." Kendrick donned his cloak and wool gloves.

"How was I supposed to know that the lass couldn't hold her ale?"

"Aye." He smirked as he teased Finn. "'Twas the ale."

Years had passed since that embarrassing night, but as any good friend would do, Kendrick made it his lifelong duty to bust Finn's ballocks about the lass who'd vomited after sleeping with him.

"For that, me friend, we're going to the tavern after work to find ye a wife." Finn grinned.

Kendrick cleared his throat. Suddenly the jesting wasn't funny anymore. Finn was serious.

———

After a long, cold day, Kendrick and Finn arrived at the tavern.

"I do believe winter will never leave," Finn complained.

"Aye, 'tis been an unusually brutal winter." Kendrick scanned the room. He'd loathed the thought of finding a wife. He relaxed some as he saw mostly men eating and drinking at the tables. The only women were too old. Perhaps he'd get away with not picking a bride!

They found an empty table and sat down.

"Yer plan is failing." Kendrick smirked. "Why would ye pick a tavern for me to find a wife?"

"Because the only lass who would have ye would be drunk."

Kendrick laughed. "Look about, there isna any women to pick from." Kendrick leaned back in his chair, gloating in victory. Tonight, he'd drink merrily without another thought of taking a wife. However, the thought of Finn executing his plan bothered him. Perplexed, Kendrick eyed his friend. "Ye weren't really going to get a lass drunk and trick her into marrying me, were ye?"

Finn grinned.

"Sometimes ye scare me, Finn."

"Ye need a wife. If we dinnae find one tonight, we'll return until we find the perfect one."

Kendrick blew out a frustrated breath. "This is a waste of time. I'm no' going to trust a stranger to come into me home." Kendrick stood. "I'm going home."

"I'm sorry to have kept ye waiting."

The sound of the sweet voice made Kendrick's heart skip a beat. Finn was peering over his shoulder with his mouth agape. "Have ye gone daft, Finn?"

"Nay, he muttered. "I've seen an angel."

Suddenly, Kendrick felt hot all over. "She's standing behind me, aye?"

Finn nodded.

No woman had that much power over a man. But Kendrick's body had indeed reacted to a voice. It was time to end Finn's game. One look at the woman should cure the lust sparking inside him. "I was just..." *Leaving?* Alluring blue eyes rendered him speechless. The lass's long red hair cascaded over her shoulders stopping at her waist. Her hips flared slightly giving her a seductive, womanly figure. Kendrick swallowed hard as he dared another look at her beautiful face. Her cheek bones were high, her lips full and red—Finn was right, she was an angel.

The lass placed two tankards down on the table. "I'm terribly sorry for the wait. The cold weather has brought in more customers hungry for our stew." She filled their cups with ale.

Kendrick stole a sniff of her hair. God's bones, she aroused him in ways he thought were long buried with Adamina.

"Are ye staying?" she asked.

Words escaped him as he stared at her.

"Aye," Finn said. "He'll be staying."

"I'll be back with yer stew." The lass smiled and winked at Kendrick before she walked away.

Inside, Kendrick was on fire. His heart, nay his cock, had risen from a long sleep. As he watched her hips sway, he imagined what it would feel like to hold her soft body against his, squeezing her round arse and kissing those sweet lips. Kendrick shook his head. *What is wrong with me?*

"Ye like her?" Finn smiled.

Kendrick took a long drink. Like wasn't the right word. He wanted to bed her, now.

"I saw the way she looked at ye."

"Finn, damn it, I'm no' taking a wife."

"She's perfect," Finn said with more excitement than Kendrick was comfortable with. "She's young."

"Stop it," Kendrick warned.

"She's kind."

Kendrick rolled his eyes.

"And she has a nice arse."

"Finn, I'm losing patience."

"I have an idea."

"Nay, no more of yer daft thinking. I'll eat me stew in peace, then I'm going home, *alone*."

"What if ye hired her to come work for ye?"

"I doubt she can plow fields and herd cattle."

"No, eejit. As a housemaid."

"I'm no' royalty. She has nothing to gain from me."

"Ye might no' be royalty, but the king has paid ye generously with land. Yer estate makes ye a verra wealthy man. So, if ye dinnae want to take a wife, hire her as yer housemaid." Finn folded his arms across his chest. "I bet she's good with children."

Kendrick glared at Finn. Between his friend's persistence, and Kendrick's overly eager physical reaction to the redheaded lass, he'd already been defeated.

4

Leana rushed into the kitchen to put some distance between her and the men at her last table. *That was too close.* No matter how hard she tried, she couldn't contain her *Baobhan sith* urges. She hadn't even realized she'd been charming those men. Her body came alive as the man with dark eyes visually undressed her. She'd imagined running her fingers through his thick hair, and she especially liked the silver streaks. A sign of an experienced man who knew how to please a woman.

Aged to perfection.

When she'd stood next to him, she could feel his heat and knew better than to look into his eyes, but she'd done it anyway. Desire swirled within his being. She'd sensed it, which intensified her craving for sex and blood.

He called to her unlike anyone before. She didn't have time to lust over a man. She had a new life and needed to stop thinking like a blood drinker and act more like a human. *What would Davina do?*

Like ashes, Leana had scattered her lies making everyone believe she was Davina, a true innocent. Why couldn't she believe it? Mayhap the urges of a blood drinker never went away.

Frustrated, Leana made her way to the hearth where a cauldron hung over the fire. She picked up a ladle and inhaled the aroma of the stew. She wrinkled her nose as the smell of garlic turned her stomach. "How could they enjoy eating this?"

"Davina."

She continued to fill the bowls.

"I know yer no' deaf."

Leana bumped into the cook.

"Lass, I've been calling yer name. Is there a reason why ye're ignoring me?"

Panicked that she's forgotten to answer to her new name, Leana quickly searched for an excuse. "I'm terribly sorry. I have a lot on me mind."

"Och, lass, get yer head out of the clouds. We have a full tavern tonight." The cook walked back to her table and uncovered two loaves of bread. "The bread is ready."

"Aye." Leana hurried over and cut two slices, putting them on a tray with the bowls of stew.

She needed to be more careful: she was Davina now.

Taking a deep breath, Leana walked into the main room, returning to the men sitting at the table. She placed the food in front of them, avoiding their gazes.

One of the men grabbed her arm as she started to go. "Wait, we'd like to talk to ye."

She turned around. "I can no'. I'm verra busy."

"Then we shall wait until yer done."

"Finn, let her go. The lass said she was busy."

Leana gazed at the man who'd stolen her breath. She recognized the pain in his eyes, the desolation. His sorrow washed over her.

"Excuse me friend," the dark-haired man said. "He means no harm."

Filled with grief, Leana couldn't speak without crying.

Finn offered her a chair. "Sit."

She did.

"I'm Finn, and this is Kendrick."

"I'm Davina."

"'Tis me pleasure." Finn kissed her hand.

"What do ye want to talk to me about?" Leana asked as she watched the men share a knowing glance.

"Opportunity," Finn simply stated.

"I have everything I want right here."

"Do ye have a husband?"

"Finn." Kendrick rolled his eyes.

Finn seemed to have something on his mind that his friend didn't want to discuss. She was intrigued enough not to walk away. "No, I dinnae have a husband."

"'Tis good." Finn grinned at Kendrick.

"Let me guess." Leana folded her arms. "One of ye are here to marry me, to offer me a happy home and children. Like I said before, I have everything I want here."

"Do ye?" Kendrick asked. "How much does the barkeep pay ye? Does he provide living quarters for ye?"

"'Tis none of yer business."

"I'd say he doesna pay ye enough to support yerself, and ye have to choose between food or clothing," Kendrick said.

Why did this man act as if he knew anything about her? His intrigue was quickly fading. "Are ye through insulting me? I must go back to work so I can afford me next meal," she said sarcastically as she stood.

Kendrick grabbed her hand. "I didnae mean to insult ye. I feel that I can give ye a better chance."

Leana slowly sat back down. Her hand tingled as he

continued to touch her fingers. What was so different about him? Like most men, he was self-assured and arrogant. She met Kendrick's dark gaze. He withdrew his hand, quickly. "Forgive me. I want ye to know my intentions are good."

"How so?" she asked.

"Finn thinks I need to hire a housemaid."

"Ye'd be perfect," Finn added.

Not knowing if she'd heard right, she questioned him. "A housemaid?"

"Kendrick is a verra wealthy man."

"Finn," Kendrick exclaimed.

"He has a large farm and servants. And children who need someone to look after them."

Kendrick shook his head, obviously opposed to what his friend was saying.

"This man was knighted on the battlefield for commanding an army with unmatched bravery," Finn continued. "The king favors him above all others."

Kendrick covered his face with both hands. "Ye dinnae know when to keep yer mouth shut."

Leana smiled.

"What's so funny?" Kendrick asked.

"The two of ye." She laughed. "Finn, ye have no shame. And Kendrick, if ye want to ask me something, just say it."

Finn sat back in the chair. "I like her."

"Davina." Kendrick faced her. "I need someone to clean me house, cook, wash and mend clothes, and tend me children. I'm willing to pay ye generously."

For a brief moment, something wicked tingled up her spine. She couldn't deny her attraction for Kendrick, nor miss the way he stared at her.

Evil follows ye.

Aye. She couldn't remember what had gone wrong at the

festival. It left a void in her memories and her heart filled with guilt. The wickedness of the night had called to her through the thinning veil between the fae and humans. Passion had been in the air and it was hers for the taking. However, she'd never expected to lose control and wake up beside two dead men. One of them Beathen, her laird's son.

The marks left behind on their necks revealed she'd been responsible for their deaths. Her sister Adaira had warned her, *"The veil is thin, Leana. The queen will send her princes for us. Stay hidden, and by the saints, dinnae draw attention to yerself."*

If she'd only listened before, Beathan would be alive.

Leana took in a deep breath. She couldn't change the past, though she desperately wanted to. The *Baobhan sith* inside her screamed to be unleashed. Yet, she reminded herself... *I am Davina. I am human.*

Leana eyed him warily. What exactly was he looking for? A wife or a woman to live with? Mayhap Kendrick was already wed.

"Does yer wife know of this arrangement?"

"Nay, she died five years ago."

"I'm sorry." Now she understood the emptiness in his eyes.

Leana considered his offer. What would Davina have done? After all, the brave lass had asked her to live life better than she had. This was the lass's prince—her new life.

Everything Kendrick offered was exactly what Leana wanted. However, there was a difference between wanting someone and needing them. Needing her meant Kendrick needed her and only her. Want...well didn't that mean he had a choice?

"Kendrick, ye said ye needed someone. Do ye want just anyone or do ye need me?"

"I want ye to accept this offer."

Leana's heart plummeted. It wasn't the response she secretly wanted. However, she wasn't giving up that easily. "I'm to accept that I'll be working as yer housemaid with wife duties without any promise of becoming yer wife. Does no' seem fair."

"I'm paying ye for a service, lass. I dinnae need a wife."

"Understood. However, I'm of marrying age. I need to find a man who at least has the intentions of marrying me."

"A handfasting?"

"Aye. I need a promise from ye that after a year of service, ye'll either marry me or let me go."

Suspicion spread across his face as he considered her proposal. "Lass, what is it that ye seek? The offer is fair."

"I seek a proper reputation. I dinnae want to dedicate me life to ye with nothing in return. I'm no' asking for much."

"Aye, ye are," Kendrick exclaimed, shoving his hands through his hair in frustration.

"Kendrick," Finn warned.

"Nay, I've offered her a deal of lifetime...to... to leave this rat hole and make a better life for herself." Kendrick stood. "I will no' be tricked into marriage."

"Sit down," Finn glared at Kendrick. "Davina is no' asking for anything unreasonable."

"Then ye marry her," Kendrick shouted.

"Ye're being rude," Finn

"I'm going home." Kendrick nodded to Leana. "'Tis been a pleasure," he said with a smirk before he walked way.

"I apologize for me friend. He's normally no' this rude."

Leana gave Finn a sideways glare. She didn't believe him.

"Aye, he's a wee bit outspoken," Finn retracted his statement.

Leana continued her glare as she crossed her arms.

"And a wee rough around the edges."

"A wee rough doesna come close."

"I should no' be telling ye this, but Kendrick is running away from some hellish demons. He loved his wife verra much and her death has devastated him."

Leana's heart softened. She knew what it was like to lose something cherished. When she'd returned to Dornoch, after escaping from the fae queen, the news of her mother's death had been hard to accept. It was even harder to stay away from her sisters.

"I'm sorry for his loss, but what does all of this have to do with me?"

"Kendrick's life is falling apart, and I can no longer watch him destroy it with his drinking. I think I've pushed him too far." Finn scrubbed his hands down his face. "I wanted to help him."

Leana touched his arm. "Ye did what any true friend would do. He must know that."

"Aye, I'm sorry to have wasted yer time, Davina." Finn stood. "I bid ye good night."

Leana watched him walk toward the door. This wasn't her problem. She didn't need to get involved, no matter how perfect an opportunity. The idea of living a normal life appealed to her. Yet, she'd not bring evil into a house with children.

Two men entered the tavern. The hair on the back of her neck stood on end. What was Bhaltair doing there, and why was he with the wolf she saved from the dark prince? *Shite!* Adaira or Masie must have sent them to find her. *This is no' good.* She couldn't let them see her.

Quickly, Leana left the table and ran after Finn before he reached the door. She pulled him into a dark corner. "Wait. I accept the offer."

Finn stared at her, confused.

"I can help Kendrick."

"Ye can?"

"Aye, and I will no' bring up marriage again. We need to leave now." Leana grabbed Finn's arm, pulling him toward the door.

"Wait. Ye should pack yer things."

"No need. I have nothing."

Finn took off his cloak and draped it over her shoulders. "Here, 'tis cold outside,"

"Thank ye." She followed him outside, looking over her shoulder to make sure Bhaltair hadn't seen her. She prayed the wolf wouldn't sniff her out.

Finn lead Leana to his horse where Kendrick waited on his own mount.

"What is this?" Kendrick asked.

"Davina has accepted yer offer."

Kendrick reached down, pulling her onto his horse.

Leana settled in front of Kendrick, keeping an eye on the tavern door. She wouldn't relax until they were far away.

"I will no' marry ye," Kendrick whispered. His breath prickled her skin in the most sinful way.

"Good," she said. "Because I dinnae want to marry ye."

Too absorbed in his own thoughts, Kendrick hadn't said a word since they'd left the tavern. Why had Davina suddenly changed her mind? Finn must have said something.

"This better no' be a trick," Kendrick warned.

"A trick?" Leana asked.

Kendrick didn't trust her. She was up to something and

had left in a rush. "I'm sure yer family will be concerned for yer safety."

Her body stiffened. "My parents died in a fire five years ago."

He shifted in the saddle, regretting his quick judgement. "I'm sorry for yer loss, lass."

"'Tis me mother I miss the most."

"Did ye have brothers or sisters?"

"My two sisters died in the fire, too."

"But ye survived."

"I wasn't home when the house burned down."

"Ye've experienced much tragedy in yer young life. I assure ye, me family will welcome ye with open arms." At least Kendrick hoped they would. "There's five tenants and their families who work for me, then Finn and his house of goats."

Davina glanced behind her, at Kendrick, her blue eyes penetrated through the gray night, warming him in ways he'd long forgotten. "Finn lives with goats?"

"Aye," Finn answered. "I have five. Fiona is by far me favorite. She's the runt of the herd but dinnae let her fool ye. She's tough. When I come home, she greets me with a cute, meeh, meeh." He smiled.

Davina laughed, but Kendrick could only imagine what was running through her mind. She must think his best friend was mad.

"Och, I happen to like me goats," Finn defended. "They are loyal animals."

"Aye, 'tis why ye live alone," Kendrick jested.

"Well, I'd love to meet yer Fiona someday," Davina said.

"I'll see to it, Davina." Finn assured her.

5

ROLLING hills covered in snow shimmered beneath the moonlight. A shadow of a house with smoke billowing from the chimney welcomed them. The smell of cattle lingered in the air with a hint of barley. In the distance, a chorus of whinnies from the horses in the barn sounded, reminding Leana of home.

Kendrick stopped in front of a stone fence and unlatched the gate. As they rode through, Leana noticed a tower. "Is this yer home?"

"Aye. 'Tis not much, but it'll keep ye safe and warm."

He dismounted and walked the horse to a small barn. Once inside, he reached up and helped Leana climb down. Their eyes met as her body slid against his. Her feet touched the ground, but why did she feel like she was floating? She should look away, break the spell. But her resistance didn't last long, she quickly admired his full lips, imagining how soft they'd feel against hers. Her eyes grew large as Kendrick leaned toward her.

Maiden, Mother, Crone, she was doing it again, compelling him to kiss her.

What was she doing? Kendrick pulled her into his arms, but she stepped out of his embrace.

"I dinnae know what came over me. I apologize for making ye feel uncomfortable. It will no' happen again." Kendrick strode out of the barn.

She caught up with him as they made their way to the tower. He left the door open as he walked inside and lit a few candles. "The children are in bed. I'll introduce ye in the morn."

Leana closed the door. The candles gave the room a soft, warm glow, inviting her into Kendrick's world.

"Please, make yerself at home," he said as he cleared the table of dirty dishes, carrying them into the kitchen.

The warmth from the hearth called to her. She walked over and placed her hands over the smoldering embers. The flames had burned out, but there was enough heat to warm her hands. She took in the room. The floor was dirty, the furniture worn, and clothes were scattered about. Indeed, Kendrick needed a maid. Above the hearth, a sword and shield covered in dust and cobwebs hung on the wall. She admired the weapons.

"They have seen much battle," Kendrick said, offering Leana a tankard of ale.

She smiled as she accepted it. "Ye should take better care of such prized possessions."

"Aye, I guess I dinnae have to use them much anymore."

"Finn mentioned ye had fought in many battles together."

Kendrick took a drink. "Aye, I fought in the king's army for many years until me wife passed."

"I'm sure ye prefer this life better, being home with yer family."

"Nay, lass. I'm a warrior, no' a farmer."

"Of course." Just looking at his muscular frame, strong weathered hands, and the small scar above his right eye, he looked a warrior. "Now that I'm here, will ye return to the king's service?"

"Nay, those days are long gone. However, I'm the fletcher for the king's army."

"With all the work on the farm, ye still make arrows for the king's archers? No wonder ye need a wife... maid."

Uncomfortable silence passed between them.

Kendrick cleared his throat. "'Tis late. I dinnae have a bedchamber prepared for ye yet. Ye can take mine for the night."

"Thank ye."

"I'll show ye to the room." Kendrick walked to the stairs, and Leana followed. They reached the third floor and followed the corridor to the end. Kendrick fumbled with the latch as he opened the door. Leana walked in. At least his chamber was cleaner than the hall.

"Everything ye need should be here." He walked over to the hearth, laying a piece of wood on the fire. "This should keep ye warm through the night."

Kendrick faced Leana, sweat breaded across his forehead. He scrubbed his hands down his trews. He was nervous; she could smell it.

"Kendrick, I'm perfectly comfortable sharing yer chamber with ye."

"Nay. I can no' allow me children to see me with a woman," he stammered.

"Where will ye sleep?"

"I'll find a spot."

"Well, at least take a fur so ye dinnae freeze." Leana grabbed one from the bed and handed it to Kendrick.

His hand brushed against hers and a swarm of

butterflies fluttered in her stomach. He was doing it again, undressing her with his eyes. Suddenly her body wasn't hers to command as she leaned toward him, wanting a kiss goodnight.

"Davina." His breath was hot against her lips. "Welcome to Lochenkirk Keep." Stepping away, he took the fur and headed toward the door.

A long sigh escaped as the door closed. Funny, she hadn't realized she'd been holding her breath. What was it about Kendrick? She crossed the chamber to the bed and fell into it with a groan. She rolled over, taking a fur with her. By the saints, he was like a warm summer's day.

A vision unfolded before her. She stood outside the keep with the wind blowing in her hair, a red-headed bairn on her hip, waiting for Kendrick to return from a long day's work plowing the fields. When he did arrive, he'd kiss her like they hadn't seen each other in days. Aye, a simple life without the threat of an evil fae queen.

Leana rolled over, clutching the fur to her chest. To think such things was a bad idea. Only fools dreamed of love. Leana sat up. Aye, she couldn't fall in love with Kendrick. It would only bring anguish and heartache to his family.

She settled back underneath the covers, smelling Kendrick on the furs and pillows. She might not be able to live out her fantasies as his wife, but nothing could keep him from her dreams.

A loud bang jolted Leanna from her sleep. "Who's there?" She looked around the chamber, seeing no one. Thinking she'd gone mad, she opened the door and stepped into the corridor. She could hear voices coming from downstairs.

Kendrick's family was awake.

With haste, she ran her fingers through her hair, braiding it. This was her first day as the housemaid and she was already late. Excitement pulsed through her as she thought about meeting Kendrick's children.

She paused at the top of the stairs, looking down into the hall.

"Da, why is there a woman in yer bedchamber?"

"Anna, 'tis no' what ye think," Kendrick told his daughter.

"Och, I believe me eyes. 'Tis one thing to put up with yer drinking and cleaning up after ye, but I will no' have ye bringing home whores. I beg ye Da, dinnae disgrace our family like this."

"Is she pretty?" a boy asked.

"Och," Anna huffed. "Kit, it does no' matter. She'll never step foot in this house again."

"Annabelle, sit down and let's talk," Kendrick said gently.

Anna did as Kendrick asked. "Please, by all that is holy, dinnae tell me ye love her and she's staying."

"Da", Kit said. "Where were ye last night?"

The youngest girl climbed onto her father's lap. Kendrick smiled and wiped her cheek. "Allie, me sweetling, when are ye going to stop growing?"

The sweet child giggled as her father tickled her.

"What did ye want to tell us?" Anna asked.

"'Tis time I hired some help around here. And I think it would be good to have a maid here, ye girls. Davina, the lass ye saw in me bedchamber, is our new housemaid."

Anna groaned.

"I thought ye'd be happy, Anna," Kendrick said.

"Nay," Anna stood. "She must go. We dinnae need a maid."

"Da," Kit interrupted. "Ye need to stop drinking. 'Tis affecting yer judgement."

"Nay", Kendrick exclaimed. "Me judgment is sound. I would no' have to ask for help if I could trust me daughter no' to sneak off at night. This has been a harsh winter and I've had to work long hours. We need a housemaid. We can no longer do it by ourselves."

"If ye'd stop spending yer time drinking, we could be a family," Anna said.

"Anna," Kit warned. "He's our father. Show some respect."

"He's a drunk," Anna said, tears running down her face.

"Anna, 'tis enough. If ye won't accept Davina then ye leave me no choice. I'll send ye to the nunnery."

Anna stood up, raising her head defiantly. "Ye disgrace mother by bringing that whore into our house. Send me away if ye must."

Anna's words hurt Leana, but she understood why they didn't want her there. They still mourned for the loss of their mother. The most surprising thing was learning of Kendrick's drinking problem.

Mayhap if Leana earned the children's trust, she could help mend their broken hearts.

Leana continued down the stairs. "Good morn."

Kendrick stood, placing Allie next to him at the table.

"Davina, this is Allie, Kit, and Anna."

"'Tis a pleasure to meet ye." Leana smiled at Allie.

"Och." Anna rolled her eyes. "Da, I want her gone." Anna donned her cloak and quit the hall.

"Ye better no' be heading to the MacTavish's," Kendrick

called after her. "Sister Elspeth will be expecting ye." Frustrated, Kendrick scrubbed his hand through his hair. "That child will be the death of me."

"'Tis nice to meet ye, Davina," Kit said, in obvious awe of Leana.

Leana grinned.

Kendrick cleared his throat. "Kit, Finn will be here soon. Ready the horses."

"Aye." Kit scooted off the bench and grabbed his cloak.

Leana cleared the table. "Ye should have wakened me. I dinnae like to be late."

"I thought ye needed rest." Kendrick followed Leana into the kitchen. "How much did ye hear?"

"Enough to know yer children dinnae want me here." Leana placed the tankards on a nearby table, then faced Kendrick. "Do *ye* want me here?"

"Aye, I made ye an offer and I stand by it."

"That's no' what I asked. Do ye *want* me here?" She searched his face, hopeful he'd say the words she longed to hear.

Kendrick shifted from one foot to the other, uncomfortable with her question. "Leana, I'm a man of me word. I would like for ye to stay."

It wasn't the exact answer she'd hoped for, but it would do for now. "Then I'll stay."

"Good. I have to go. Finn and Kit are waiting for me."

Leana followed Kendrick out of the kitchen and into the hall. He kissed Allie. "I almost forgot. Watch over the wee one. She likes to hide."

Allie smiled innocently.

"Sir Kendrick, dinnae fash yerself. I'm sure Allie will be too busy for tricks." Leana returned Allie's mischievous grin.

After Kendrick left, Leana sat down with Allie who was finishing her porridge. "Where should we start today?"

"The kitchen," Allie said as she slid off the bench, taking her bowl with her. "Anna always complains about the dishes."

Leana looked at the dirty tankards and trenchers piled high on the table. They'd need to make a trip to the stream to wash all those dishes. "Allie, is there a stream nearby?"

Allie nodded.

"Good. Help me fill the cart with the dirty dishes and help me wash them. Once we finish, I promise to play with ye."

Allie looked up at Leana, then grimaced at the pile of dishes. "That is one beast ye can no' slay alone."

"Stay here, I'll fetch the cart," Leana said.

"The cart is right outside the door."

Once the dishes were loaded in the cart, Leana helped Allie with her cloak, put on her own, then they went outside.

"Da hooks the cart up to his horse."

"Och, child, yer da has his horse. We'll make do. How far is the stream?"

"No' far." Allie pointed.

Leana walked to the front of the cart and picked up the shafts. With a hefty pull, she and Allie were headed to the stream.

After spending the greater part of the morn washing dishes, Allie kept her promise and helped Leana put the dishes away. "This is the last trencher," Allie said with a smile.

"Thank ye, lass." Leana suspected the wee lass was up to something. "What's that smile for?"

Allie bounced up and down excitedly. "Ye promised to play."

Leana blew out an exhausted breath. "Aren't ye tired?'

"Nay," Allie giggled. "I'll hide and ye'll find me." Allie ran out of the kitchen.

"Allie, wait," Leana called after her, but she had already disappeared. "Maiden, Mother, Crone." Leana chased the lass upstairs. "Allie, I will find ye."

Leana breathed in the air, using her superior senses to hone in on Allie's unique scent. Aye, she was cheating, but no one would ever find out. Leana closed her eyes and took another breath. Within seconds, she smelled heather. Leana opened her eyes and continued to a bedchamber.

She opened the door. "I found ye," she called into the dark.

Allie's soft laughter made her smile.

Leana grabbed a torch off the wall as she entered the chamber. "I know ye're in here Allie." She lit a few candles. Dust covered table tops and the hearth looked as if it hadn't been used in years. The bed was covered with furs. Who did this chamber belong to?

A rustling noise from the wardrobe made Leana think the child was hiding inside. "Allie," she whispered. *Sly lass.* She crept to the heavy piece of furniture and swung the doors open. "Got ye!" But she didn't find Allie. She moved the dresses aside. "Where are ye?"

Leana took a step back, gazing at the garments. She ran her hand across them and stopped at a green dress. Mesmerized by its beauty, she took it out and held it up, admiring the intricate pattern of pearls down the sleeves.

She'd never seen a prettier one. She laid the dress against her body. "'Tis a perfect fit." She had to try it on.

Forgetting about Allie, she tried the dress on. It hugged her body in all the right places.

"Ye look beautiful."

Leana turned around.

"Can I put one on, too?" Allie walked to the wardrobe.

"Wait, Allie." Leana tried to stop her but it was too late. Allie had pulled a dress out. "I dinnae think this is a good idea."

Allie folded her arms. "Ye put one on."

Leana was defenseless against the lass's pleading face. "Only one," she warned.

The lass squealed with joy as Leana helped her into the dress. Allie twirled around. "I feel like a princess. Mother must have looked beautiful in this dress."

Mother? Everything came together, the tidy bedchamber and beautiful gowns, all of it belonged to Kendrick's dead wife. "Aye. But we should no' be in yer mum's bedchamber."

"I know," Allie averted her gaze. "But this room is all I have to remind me of her."

Leana studied Allie for a moment. The lass needed to feel close to her mum; she couldn't deprive her of that. "We can stay, but not for long."

For the next few hours, Allie tried on dresses and jewelry found in one of the trunks.

"Allie, if ye hang another chain around yer neck, ye'll fall over." Leana chuckled.

"Aren't they pretty?" Allie twirled around, showing off the long strands of pearls and gems.

"Och, come over here and I'll pin yer hair up to show off yer fine treasures." Leana grabbed a comb, sat down, and patted the mattress.

Allie danced over and plopped down. As she combed through the mass of red tangled hair, Leana hummed a familiar tune.

"'Tis pretty," Allie said.

"Aye. When I was yer age, me mum sang to me while brushing me hair. It was always a tangled mess, so I hated having it brushed. Me mum sang to me to ease the pain."

Allie looked down into her lap. "I never met me mum. She died when I was born."

Sorrow grew inside Leana's chest. She felt sorry for the lass, for there wasn't a night that had gone by that Leana hadn't thought about her mother. The blood oath Leana had sworn came with grave consequences. She hadn't been there when her mother needed her most.

For the last ten years, Leana had lived without a mother. The fae queen was a poor substitute, her heart too dark and cold to ever love anyone, not even a ten-year old child. Every day she'd missed her mum and wished she was back in Dornoch in her bedchamber with her mum brushing her hair and singing to her.

Leana's heart raced as she recalled a time she'd stupidly disobeyed the queen's orders. It hadn't been the first time she'd challenged the queen, but it was last time she'd taken the queen for a fool...

At ten and six, Leana had been rewarded with a seat on the royal fae court next to her older sister, Adaira. The new role had come with power, which influenced Leana to speak her mind too often. Especially when it came to her younger sister Masie.

The queen took advantage.

A council meeting had been called, and Leana felt braver than usual as she waited for the queen to speak.

Adaira knew Leana wished to rebel. "Whatever nonsense ye

have inside yer head, 'tis best to remain silent. The queen is in a foul mood today."

Leana grinned. "Fear not, sister. I'll be good."

The meeting began, and the Seelie fae were asking for protection against a neighboring human clan. Their mound was in grave danger.

Leana fought to keep her eyes open—she didnae care. They had been discussing the same concern for over an hour. Maiden, Mother, Crone, please, someone put a stop to it.

The room grew eerily quiet, and Leana looked up. Queen Snowdrop raised her hand, stopping further rants. "Are we boring you, child? Should the realm fool be brought in for your entertainment?" The queen's fiery, dark eyes burned holes in Leana's soul.

The queen could hear her thoughts. Leana stared back at her. She stood, ignoring her sister's warning to sit back down. "We've heard the problem over and over. Does anyone have a solution?"

The queen tapped her long, black nails against the armrest of her throne "This is my council and I'll proceed as I see fit."

Leana frowned and sat, silent.

Once the meeting concluded, the queen motioned for one of her fae princes to bring her something. Fear stirred in Leana's stomach, she sensed danger—a very personal kind.

Alder escorted Masie to the queen.

"Nay," Leana gasped.

"My daughter, my sweet Masie." The queen stood with outstretched arms, welcoming Masie.

"Adaira," Leana whispered. "I do no' like this. What is the queen up to?"

"I dinnae know."

The queen always struck with purpose, which made Leana nervous. Whatever she had planned, there'd be no mercy.

"I have decided it's time for Masie to have an escort."

"Nay, this can no' be happening." Leana's chest tightened as she thought of the worst possible reason for Masie to be presented to the council. She was too young to attend court. However, it was common practice for Unseelie girls to have a male escort. They served as their protectors. Once a girl reached maturity, the escort had the right to claim the girl.

Leana had witnessed this firsthand with Adaira. She'd been promised to Ash. A horrible mistake. The union had never taken place, and Ash was lucky to escape with his ballocks still attached.

However, Leana was supposed to be next, Masie wasn't of age. Mayhap she'd been worried about nothing. But her stomach still churned with fear. The queen's threats were never baseless.

"Today you become a lady." The queen looked down at Masie.

The fae parted, opening a pathway to the queen. Aspen strutted past Leana, smiling as he joined the queen. This couldn't be happening.

"Masie, I present your escort, Aspen, a son of the Ice Crystal Plains."

Nay, Masie is only ten and three!

Leana met the queen's dark gaze. The challenge in her eyes provoked Leana to speak.

"My queen, she's but a child. As her sister, I can no' allow ye to do this."

The queen's gaze narrowed, and Leana knew she'd crossed the line. With one flick of the queen's hand, the room cleared, leaving only Leana. "Who are you to defy my orders? I am your queen, your mother."

"Ye are no' me mother."

With graceful steps, the queen descended from her dais and approached Leana. "I admire your sprit, child. It matches your fire-kissed hair."

"Ye can no' do this to Masie. 'Tis me ye want to punish."

The queen grabbed Leana's chin. "You have pushed me too far. I don't understand why you constantly disobey me. I have given you everything you've asked for. Doughall is dead, your mother's freedom is assured, yet you still treat me as if I'm your enemy."

Fixed upon the queen's vexed glare, Leana showed no fear.

The queen frowned and let go of Leana's chin, sighing. "Ye took advantage of three wee lassies and tricked us into a blood oath. Ye did us no' favors. We never asked to be blood drinkers."

"And yet you accepted my gift."

"We had no choice."

"Your mother kept something precious from you and your sisters. She never told you about your special gifts, did she?"

"What do you mean?"

"Your mother is a Seelie fae. You are Seelie." The queen ran the back of her hand down Leana's cheek, the coldness of the touch made her shiver. "Seelies bring light to summer and spring. Their light holds the purest magic."

"I dinnae believe ye. Yer my aunt, wouldn't ye be a Seelie?"

"I was. But I saw the power in the Unseelie and pledged my life to them. Yer mother stole something very important to me. Without it, my world fell to darkness."

Leana's head was spinning; she didn't know what to believe. "All along, ye used me sisters and I to hurt me mother?"

"Someone had to pay for my broken heart. She took my true love, so I took hers." The queen rubbed her hands together, then opened them in front of her. Black smoke curled around her fingertips. She waved her hands in a circle until a black cloud formed, then blew into the cloud.

"What is this?"

"Look deeper, my child."

Lightening streaked across the dark clouds, followed by room-shaking thunder. A flash of blue light shot from the darkness and into Leana's eyes. She squinted against the intensity of the light and tried to look away but couldn't. What was the queen doing to her?

Panicked, Leana begged. "Please stop."

"Remember, you did this to your mother." The queen walked away.

An image of her mother standing on the edge of the cliffs of Dornoch with their clan plaid wrapped around her shoulders appeared. The sea breeze whipped violently through her hair and dress. Leana could taste the salty air and feel the ocean mist on her skin as if she was standing next to her mother. "Mum," she whispered as she reached into the cloud.

As if her mother heard her, she turned around. Exhaustion marked her mother's beautiful face. Sadness had replaced the sparkle in her eyes. Her red hair was streaked with silver.

Leana wept uncontrollably. She'd done this to her mother. "Mum, I'm here. Masie and Adaira are here. We're coming home."

Leana watched her mother slowly turn around, the plaid slipped from her shoulders and blew away, disappearing over the cliff. Her mum took a step forward.

"Nay," Leana shouted. "We're coming home." She fought to close her eye, but the light was too powerful. She fought against the queen's spell, but it was useless. "Please, Mum, dinnae jump."

Horrified, Leana watched helplessly as her mother stepped off the cliff and plummeted to the rocky shoreline.

Leana was immediately broken. She'd felt her mother's pain. All that sorrow had come from losing her children. If Leana could only turn back time to the day she saw the fairy fire, she wouldn't have followed it into the glen.

The queen had finally discovered her weakness, Leana's beloved mother. And her evil aunt had finally broken Leana's spirit.

Allie tugged on Leana's sleeve, breaking the spell.

"Davina, is there something wrong?"

The ache in Leana's chest screamed to be released. She wanted to tell the lass everything, but couldn't.

"Me mother passed when I was young, too. I know how much ye must miss yer mum."

"Anna and Kit tell me stories about her. Da will no' talk about her. Do ye have sisters or brothers?"

"I have two..." Quickly, Leana stopped herself from revealing the truth. She wasn't Leana anymore, she was Davina. The past didnae matter. "I only knew me mum."

Allie's blue eyes pierced Leana's heart as the lass took her hand. "Ye have a family now."

Something buried deep inside Leana surfaced. She'd long forgotten what it felt like to be shown kindness. She wrapped her arms around Allie.

"What is going on here?" Anna rushed into the chamber. "What are ye wearing?"

Allie jumped off the bed and ran to her sister. "Anna, please dinnae tell Da."

"Ye know ye're no' allowed in mother's bedchamber." Anna threw Leana a hate-filled glare. "Ye should know better. Once Father finds out, he'll throw ye out."

"Anna, no harm was done." Leana walked to Allie.

"Ye're wearing me mother's dress?" Anna exclaimed.

Leana looked down at the beautiful gown. "I'm sorry."

"There's nothing to be sorry for, Davina," Allie said. "Ye did nothing wrong."

"Allie, take that dress off and leave this room," Anna scolded.

"Anna, I think ye're overreacting," Leana said.

"Overreacting?" Anna stood with a hand braced on her hip. "I come home and a stranger is in me mother's bedchamber wearing her clothes. What am I supposed to think?"

"Allie hid in here while we were playing."

"Nay," Allie said as she put her own dress on. "Ye didnae find me. I found ye."

Leana smiled at the wee lass, then looked back to Anna. "Yer father has entrusted me with taking care of all of ye."

"Och, me da is a drunk."

"Ye should no' talk about yer da that way, lass. He puts a roof over yer head and food in yer stomach."

"Stop trying to be me mother," Anna yelled. "I do no' care why ye're in here, just get out."

"Anna," Leana pleaded. "I'm no' the enemy."

Leana raced downstairs, escaping Anna's harsh tongue. Being scolded by a child was humiliating. She didn't deserve it. She reached the great hall and paced in front of the hearth. She was angry...nay, furious with Anna's behavior. All she wanted was acceptance. She wasn't there to replace Adamina. If only she could find a way to get that through Anna's stubborn mind.

Leana swiped a tear from her cheek. "Och, a child has made me weep."

"Davina."

She turned around, and Kendrick was staring at her. Realization washed over her as she remembered she was still wearing Adamina's dress.

Appalled that she'd forgotten to take it off, Leana pleaded, "I can explain, Kendrick."

"Nay." He walked over and tucked her hair behind her ears, giving him a clearer view of the dress. "Ye look beautiful." His gaze roamed over her body, igniting something wicked deep inside her.

Keep the beast under control, Leana.

Nervously, Kendrick cleared his throat. "I mean...the dress...the dress is beautiful."

"I'm sorry. I was playing with Allie and she hid in your wife's bedchamber. I didnae know—"

"Davina." Kendrick helped her into a chair. "Sit. Breathe."

She met his gaze, a calming sensation washing over her.

"What happened today? Did Allie cause ye trouble?"

Still not able to talk, Leana shook her head.

"Anna?"

Leana nodded.

"She has pushed me too far." Kendrick strode to the staircase and called for his daughter. "Anna Fletcher, come down here!"

"Nay," Leana muttered. "I will be fine."

"The lass needs to apologize."

"Kendrick, it will only make matters worse. 'Tis my fault. Anna walked in while Allie and I were trying on yer wife's clothes. I should no' have allowed it."

Kendrick walked back to the hearth. He scrubbed a hand down his face. "She saw that?"

"Aye."

Kendrick exhaled.

"It was awful."

Kendrick knelt in front of Leana and held her shaking hands. "I apologize for her behavior. I know her words can sting. 'Tis been difficult for her. However, that does no' excuse her rude behavior."

Leana gazed into his eyes. He was genuinely embarrassed by his daughter.

"I understand the pain she's feeling. There's no' a day that goes by that I dinnae miss me mum." Leana stared at their joined hands. "I didnae know how hard this would be."

"'Tis only yer first day and I've never seen the kitchen so clean."

"Allie helped." A smile spread across her face. "She's a wonderful child."

"Aye." Kendrick tipped her chin up with his finger. "Ye're smiling. This is good, aye?"

"Aye." Leana's smile brightened.

"Please, dinnae give up on us."

Did her ears deceive her? He wanted her to stay? "I dinnae break that easily." She met his gaze. "I'm no' leaving."

6

ADAIRA SLIPPED FROM THE BED, careful not to wake her wolf. Rafe rolled over, giving her pause. She stared at his handsome face. Her wolf was truly an angel; one look and she was under his spell. For a moment she wanted to crawl back into bed with him. But she had much to accomplish.

Since Bhaltair and Teg had left in search of Leana, an unsettling fear had taken root inside Adaira. It made her restless. Leana had been gone too long. And why hadn't the men found her yet? Had the queen captured them? Was Leana her prisoner, too?

Suddenly feeling sick to her stomach, she knelt beside the bed and grabbed the chamber pot. She threw up three times.

Catching her breath, she sat back on her heels, wiping her mouth with the back of her hand. She had to find Leana. If Bhaltair and Teg didn't bring Leana home soon, she'd go herself.

Rafe's gentle snore broke, and Adaira gazed at her husband. *"Please, dinnae let him be awake."* He couldn't see her this way, naked and kneeling on the floor next to the chamber pot. How was she going to explain herself without causing him to panic? Thankfully, her husband still slept.

By the gods, she hated keeping things from Rafe. Her sickness was nothing to worry about. The time to attack the queen grew closer, and every day that passed without word from Leana, the stomach pains and nausea worsened. Besides, Rafe knew her fears, there was no need to keep reminding him. She could take care of herself.

Adaira pushed herself up from the floor and walked to the wash basin. She washed her face and hands, then dressed. Feeling better, she left the bedchamber.

Adaira made her way to the kitchens. She grabbed a pitcher of wine and tankard, then sat down in the great hall. It was late; no one was milling around, so she had the privacy she needed to think about the attack. The queen needed to be dealt with before she set her eyes on Dornoch. Adaira sensed Queen Snowdrop's hunger for revenge, the need to control everything.

The sound of small footsteps pattered down the stairs. Adaira didn't need to look up to see who joined her.

Adaira ran her finger around the rim of the cup. "I can no' remember the last time I've seen the sun."

Masie sat down next to her.

"I fear we'll never see it again."

"Och, sister," Masie said. "We will overcome the darkness. We'll find Leana and take back our freedom from the queen. We must." Masie held her hand over her stomach.

Adaira's eyes widened as she looked at her sister's swollen belly. "Ye're with child."

"Aye." Masie grinned. "Ina says 'tis a boy." Masie's grin faded. "And a blood drinker."

Stunned, Adaira didn't know what to say. Their kind

couldn't bear children; or so she had thought. "Can Ina be trusted?"

Masie stood. "I dinnae know who to trust anymore. I believe her, for I can feel him inside me. I want to be happy, but I fear Ina is right. He's a blood drinker."

"Masie, have ye told Kerr?"

"Aye."

"And..."

"He's overjoyed to have a son."

"Do ye believe him?"

"Aye." Masie's brows creased. "He's the only one I trust completely."

Adaira knew what Masie was hinting at. Unresolved trouble lingering between them. "Masie, I had to leave ye in Ravens Landing. It was the only way to keep ye safe."

"Nay. Leana and ye abandoned me. Do ye know how terrified I was? I thought I'd never see ye again."

"If ye want me to apologize, I will no'. I kept ye safe."

Masie stood with her hands folded over her chest. "I do no' want to fight. Ye knew I would no' have approved of yer plan. We should have talked about it."

"Aye," Adaira agreed.

"Ye're agreeing to keep me happy. I know ye Adaira Keith, ye're as stubborn as a mule."

After a shared moment of laughter, the dark cloud of doubt returned. How could they escape their uncertain future?

"Adaira, have faith. Bhaltair and Teg will find Leana."

"Ye sound like Rafe." Adaira sighed in annoyance.

"He's a wise wolf. Trust him."

Adaira looked at her sister and smiled. Masie always saw the good in people. Her faith never wavered even through tough times. However, Adaira didn't share Masie's belief.

The danger ahead wasn't something to take lightly. The odds were against them.

Suddenly, a gust of wind blew the castle door open. A violent swirl of snow and ice filled the room, and Adaira moved toward the door, shielding her face with her arm. Surprisingly, Bhaltair and Teg appeared.

"Bhaltair," Masie exclaimed.

"Teg," Adaira called out, pleased to see him.

"Where's Leana?" Adaira asked.

"We found her." Bhaltair removed his gloves.

Panicked, Adaira thought the worst. Was Leana dead? Fear gripped her heart and she couldn't speak.

"Where is she?" Masie asked as she took Bhaltair's cloak.

Teg shook his head like a wet dog. "We found her at a tavern, a two-day ride north of here."

Relief and joy filled Adaira. Her sister was alive. "Why didn't she come with ye?"

The men gazed at each other as Masie escorted them to the fire. "It was too risky."

"What do ye mean?" Adaira asked.

"I wanted to bring her home," Teg said. "But Bhaltair threatened to take me manhood if I disobeyed a direct order."

Adaira turned to Bhaltair. "What?"

"Let me explain," Bhaltair said.

"I ordered ye to bring me sister home." It'd be a miracle if Bhaltair left the great hall with his head still attached. "Ye'd better have a damn good reason for leaving me sister behind."

"Och, if ye kill me, ye'll never find out." Bhaltair stepped forward; a fool for challenging her.

"Adaira," Masie warned, stepping between them. "I'm sure there's a good reason."

"We tracked Leana to a tavern like Teg said. She left there with two men."

Adaira rolled her eyes. "Apparently Leana hasn't learned her lesson."

Masie glared at her. "She's our sister."

Teg cleared his throat, gaining Adaira's attention. "'Tis not what ye think. She's living with a family on a farm."

"What?" Adaira asked. "This still does no' excuse the fact ye left her there."

"I made the decision to leave her because I dinnae have the power nor strength to make Leana leave. A wolf is no match for a *Baobhan sith*. I didnae what to scare her and have her run away."

Bhaltair was right. Knowing her sister, she would've bolted if she felt threatened. Adaira took a deep breath.

"Can I speak freely?" Bhaltair asked.

Adaira nodded.

"I believe 'tis best ye go to her."

"Over my dead body," a voice growled from the stairs.

Adaira met Rafe at the bottom of the staircase. "They found Leana."

"Aye," Rafe kissed her forehead. "Ye'll not go on yer own."

"I'll be with her," Masie said.

Adaira faced Masie. "No' in yer condition."

"I'm well enough to ride a horse."

"And what condition are ye in?" Bhaltair asked.

"I'm pregnant."

Bhaltair raced to Masie's side. "Yer with child? Does me brother know?"

"Aye," Masie said. "Of course, he does."

"He willna let ye go," Bhaltair said.

"Enough," Adaira exclaimed. "I'm going." She looked at Rafe. "Alone."

"My queen," Rafe stated sternly. "I'm going with ye."

Adaira didn't need anyone slowing her down. "Ye're a stubborn wolf."

Teg stepped forward. "I'm going, too."

"Me, too," Masie insisted.

"No' without me." Masie's husband, Kerr, entered the great hall. "That's me child," he stood in front of Masie and rubbed her belly. "I will protect him with me life."

Masie looked up at Kerr, then whispered, "Thank ye."

Speechless, Adaira shook her head. Her family and servants obviously loved her. How could she deny their help? However, the fear churning in her stomach was still there. With the fae queen still a threat, the journey to recover Leana could be dangerous.

"Och, sister," Masie said as she kissed Adaira's cheek. "I told ye to have faith."

7

KENDRICK DISMOUNTED FROM HIS HORSE, thankful he was finally home. Another hour in the frigid snow and he would've frozen to death. Fixing up the old barn in the middle of the coldest winter he'd ever lived through was going to send him to an early grave. However, the project was a good distraction from what was happening at home.

It had been too long since Kendrick had been welcomed home with warm meals, clean clothes, and a tidy house. He hated that Finn had been right. His family needed Davina. After a chaotic few weeks, his kids had finally warmed up to her. However, he fought to keep himself in check. Having a woman in his house stirred old memories back to life, releasing feelings that had been buried long ago.

Davina was beautiful; he'd be a fool not to notice her curves, full lips, and her long, red hair. Many nights after the ale had numbed his mind, he'd lie in bed and imagine what it would be like to tangle his fingers in those locks as he pulled her into a kiss. If she warmed his bed as well as she cooked, he be a lucky man.

Like his wife, Davina was patient and kind; even when

Anna argued for no reason. Kit was bewitched by Davina's beauty. And Allie...sweet wee Allie took to Davina like she'd found a new friend.

Davina was a blessing...as long as he steered away from temptation.

Kendrick paused before opening the door as the smell of freshly baked bread filled his senses. He closed his eyes and inhaled. *Damn.* His cock strained against his trews. Good food went straight to his heart.

Kendrick opened the door. Davina and Allie were sitting on a chair in front of the hearth, reading a book together.

"The...pah...pah..." Allie struggled as she tried to read.

"Princess," Davina corrected.

"Princess Mar..."

"Marjorie," Davina said.

"Princess Marjorie Bruce," Allie exclaimed joyfully.

"Aye, ye're reading verra well, lass."

Kendrick tore his eyes away from them. There was nothing sweeter in the world. He shut the door and cleared his throat, making sure his presence was known.

"Da!" Allie jumped off Davina's lap.

Kendrick picked Allie up. "And how's me princess of Lochenkirk Keep?"

"Davina has been teaching me to read."

Kendrick's body heated as Davina joined them.

"Aye, we've been reading about King Robert and the battles he won for freedom."

"Ye're reading a book about battles?" Kendrick's brows creased as he looked at Allie.

"Aye, Da. He was a great warrior. Just like ye."

"And yer grandfather." Kendrick put Allie down and dared a glance at Davina.

"Ye should add a few fables fitted for the lass to yer reading collection," Davina said. "She's a strong reader."

"Aye, too wise for her own good," Kendrick joked as he patted the top of Allie's head.

"Och, I almost forgot." Allie ran to the kitchen.

"Allie," Davina called after her. "Be careful. It still might be hot."

Davina helped Kendrick out of his cloak and stepped away before she touched him. He walked over to the table, poured himself some ale, downed it, then poured another. "I'll be in me workshop."

"Wait," Davina followed him to the door. "Allie made something for ye."

"I have a lot of work to do."

"Kendrick..."

He shut the door before Leana could say another word.

Feeling like a compete arse, Kendrick threaded a feather onto the end of the arrow he was making. It was the twentieth one he'd fletched in less than an hour, and it was only his second pitcher of ale. Seeing Davina with Allie threatened his peace of mind; he wanted a new life, wanted to love again, but didn't know how.

Adamina would have approved of Davina, for happiness was slowly being restored in his house. However, there was a wall surrounding his heart, preventing him to love freely.

Why did he feel so damn guilty for bringing Davina into his home?

Because ye heart still belongs to Adamina.

Shaking off his thoughts, Kendrick inspected the shaft of the arrow. He ran his hand down it, admiring the sound craftsmanship. Made from ancient pines in a sacred forest, the wood was unlike any other. It was blessed with Druid magic.

There was a reason the men in his family were born with the passion for battle and the taste for blood. He came from a long line of powerful Druids. Though their numbers had slowly dwindled, their magic thrived.

Someone knocked on the door. "Kendrick."

He stopped threading the feather. *For all that's holy, lass, go away.*

Davina stepped inside.

Shite.

"I brought ye a piece of bread Allie made." She placed a plate on his workbench. "I promised Allie I'd make sure ye got some."

Ignoring her, Kendrick continued working on the arrow.

"Would it hurt ye to say thank ye?"

"Thank ye," he mumbled just to make her happy, so she'd go away.

But she didn't move.

Leana leaned in, and he froze as the plaid she wore slide off her shoulder. Flesh pure as fresh-fallen snow was inches from his touch. His throat went dry.

"Allie worked verra hard on the bread. The next time ye see her, tell her how proud ye are. She's a bright child with a kind heart. Dinnae break it," Davina said.

Kendrick tossed the arrow on the work bench. What did she know about raising a family? He stood. "Do ye have children?"

Davina retreated a step. "I...I dinnae. Ye know that."

"Then why would I take yer advice?"

"Because it does no' take a wise man to see what's happening here. Ye're pushing yer children away. Ye come home from work and head straight to this shop. When was the last time ye sat down and ate a meal with yer family?"

"Davina, my family is no' yer concern."

"Och, ye hired me to take care of them. They are me responsibility. Did ye know Anna is learning to sew, and Allie loves to read?"

"I'm no'..." Kendrick couldn't finish his sentience under Davina's scrutiny.

"Nay. Ye dinnae know, because every night ye lock yerself in this shop avoiding yer family."

"Stop acting like me wife."

"Och, someone has to be honest with ye."

The lass was out of line—or was she?

Through the anger, Kendrick didn't realize how close he was to Davina until he'd pinned her against the wall. He met her challenging gaze. The lass wasn't scared of him, but he sure as hell was afraid of her.

Davina drew him in like a moth to a flame.

"I know what ye want, Kendrick," she whispered, her breath hot against his cheek.

"Ye know nothing." He met her gaze. "I will no' fall for yer trickery."

Davina grinned like the devil. "Ye've already fallen."

She was familiar, yet he didn't know her. What was happening to him? He yearned to touch her. To taste her. Aye, there was something different about this lass. He could feel it. This wasn't ordinary lust, it reeked of magic.

With a hunger he could no longer control, he claimed her lips. Sweet and hot like warm honey, his tongue thrust into her mouth. She pulled him closer, her firm breasts pressed against his chest. His heart raced with excitement. This had to stop before there was no turning back.

Kendrick broke the kiss. Out of breath, Davina looked up at him and smiled.

"Who are ye," he asked, bewildered at how his body responded to Davina.

"I can no' tell ye all me secrets." Davina ducked underneath his arms and darted out of the shop.

Kendrick stared at the door, reliving that fateful kiss. Aye, there was a part of him that wanted her to stay. However, he wasn't one to allow his cock to overrule his common sense. Untamed passion left him craving more. Companionship. Laughter. Love.

But it wasn't right. He'd pledged his heart to his wife.

Kendrick freed himself from Davina's spell. "Nay, this can no' be." He wiped her kiss from his mouth as he walked over and grabbed a tankard of ale. He downed it and refilled his cup over and over again, ingesting so much the room spun out of control. The way Davina had made him feel inside.

Kendrick slammed his hands on the table. He hardly possessed the strength to hold his body up. His shoulders drooped in defeat. "Adamina," he whispered.

The door to the shop blew open and a gust of frigid air filled the room. He turned toward the door. "Davina?"

The cloud of snow disappeared and he expected to see the red-haired lass, but no one was there. He pushed off the table and walked outside, pausing as the wind blew over his body. A sweet voice he knew all too well called to him. "Adamina." He squinted though the flurries, confused. Even though he saw nothing, something within the wind called his name.

"Kendrick."

Her sweet voice sounded real. He shook his head, fighting the cruel trickery. *Nay, she's gone, Kendrick.*

The pain was too much. Kendrick gave in and followed the voice through the forest. He knew exactly where it was leading him, for he visited the place often.

The voice stopped as he reached a small clearing. A blanket of snow covered the ground. Even the fire pit he'd built next to the grave was hidden. He bent over and brushed the stones clean until a rectangular outline was visible.

He straightened, looking down at the grave. A small part of a cross that laid flat inside the stones was visible. Kendrick knelt and wiped the rest of the snow away. He sat back on his heels. The ache in his chest grew. "I'm so sorry. I've made a mess out of our lives. Ye were the string that binded our family together. Without ye, Adamina, me life is falling apart."

A stick figure next to the cross caught his eye. He walked over and pulled it from the snow. *A doll?* He dusted the rest of the snow off it. *How did it get there?*

As he examined the doll, he noticed the twigs were gold with a wavy grain. *A yew tree.* Kendrick smiled. He knew exactly who had put this on his wife's grave.

Not too long ago, he'd explained to Anna the meaning of the ancient yew tree and the power it held. He shared when the yew was placed on a grave, it was a reminder that death was only a pause in life before rebirth.

Kendrick placed the doll on top of the cross. *Rebirth?* Aye, if only true. If only those sticks would magically bring Adamina back. His heart broke knowing how much Anna wanted her mother back.

Kendrick fell to his knees. Why had she been taken from him? He'd failed to keep his family together. He'd failed at being a father. Adamina was his better half. She made him a better man. If it hadn't been for her, he would've died a long time ago.

And now that he'd felt what love was, he didn't want to let her go. He'd never understand why the gods took such a fine woman away from him...away from his children. Aye, he'd cursed the gods may times.

Mayhap, the gods were punishing him for all the killing he'd done. Maybe she had died because of him.

Tears burned his eyes, his chest tightened as anger bubbled into rage. He threw his head back and yelled into the night sky like a howling wolf. "Why," he cried, years of hurt bleeding out of his soul.

A ray of light shined down on his body, warming him. Bewildered, he reached for the beam. Light glowed through his hand

Adamina's voice returned. "Kendrick."

Calmness washed over him.

Kendrick opened his eyes to see the light streak across the sky. "Adamina," he whispered as he collapsed in the snow.

8

LEANA TRIED to make sense of everything as she paced restlessly in her bedchamber. She couldn't forget Kendrick's kiss. Her body hummed with need and curiosity. No man had ever made her feel like this, especially from a kiss.

"Who are ye, Kendrick the Fletcher?"

No mortal should be as dangerously handsome as Kendrick. The ancient gods must have cast him from stone. Sucking in a shaky breath, she remembered how strong his body felt pressed against her. What did his body look like underneath that tunic?

Maiden, Mother, Crone. She could no longer ignore the exhilarating pull he had over her.

She liked her new home. She'd grown to care for his children. And for the first time in some years, she felt like she had a purpose in life. That she belonged...that she was needed. The children saw her as a normal woman, not a creature that nightmares were made of.

They will find out. Leave now before it's too late.

Nay. This was no time for irrational thoughts. She wasn't going to live in fear. She had to know Kendrick's true self, and if that meant she had to tell him the truth about everything, well, that was a risk she'd take. No more lies.

Determined to change her future, Leana walked out of her bedchamber to find Kendrick. She took the stairs with haste before she changed her mind. Something told her that the truth was going to hurt both of them, but who would suffer the most?

Leana grabbed her cloak before leaving the keep. She treaded through the thick snow to Kendrick's workshop. He was always in his shop. "Kendrick," she called.

When he didn't answer, Leana opened the door and stepped inside. "We need to talk." She turned to shut the door and her body froze, for she knew there was no turning back. She had to tell him the truth. "Kendrick, I know ye are something more than ye say. I felt it in yer touch. Tell me yer secret, and I'll share mine."

Her brows creased in confusion. He wasn't here. "Kendrick." She searched the shop. *Where could he be?*

Thinking he might have snuck inside the keep without her knowing, Leana left the shop. As she began to walk back to the keep, she noticed a trail of footprints in the snow leading toward the back of the keep. "What was he doing out in the snow? Daft man will freeze his ballocks off."

Leana followed the trail and stopped at the tree line where the footprints disappeared into the forest. Her inner voice warned her not to go any further. But Kendrick was out there, and he needed her; she felt it.

"Kendrick!" She braved the first few steps into the dark woods, listening for him. She heard a faint heartbeat. But why was he so weak?

Horrified that something bad had happened, Leana ran to a clearing, stopping at a grave. "Kendrick..." She fell to her knees and pulled him onto her lap. She brushed the snow from his face. "Wake up, ye eejit." There was no need to check for a pulse. She'd eyed the thick vein running down his neck. He was alive, barely.

"Kendrick ye will no die on me. Allie needs ye. Wake up." She slapped his face.

Moaning, he opened his eyes. "Davina?"

She wrinkled her nose at the smell of sour ale on his breath. "By the gods, Kendrick, how much have ye been drinking?"

"Not enough. I'm still alive."

"Och, ye fool." She pushed him away.

"Bloody hell, lass," he moaned as he rolled to his side, in obvious pain.

Leana stood, disgusted. "What are ye doing to yerself? This is no way for a father to act."

"I dinnae need ye to tell me that. I know." Kendrick sat up, brushing snow off his clothes.

As much as it angered her to see Kendrick like this, she understood everyone had demons to slay. His were fighting relentlessly. Who was she to judge? She bent down next to him. "Talk to me, Kendrick." She cupped his face. "Yer demons are too strong to fight alone. Let me help ye."

Kendrick turned away angrily. "What do ye know of demons?" He pushed up from the ground and stood. "Dinnae talk to me about something ye know nothing about."

Leana faced him. "A wise man knows when he needs help."

"I dinnae need yer help."

He didn't need her help. He was too far gone. However, her feelings wouldn't let her go.

Leana joined Kendrick at the grave. "Is this the ghost ye've been fighting?"

"Aye," he said grimly. "She's me wife."

Leana didn't know what to say. She had a different view on death than humans, and no matter how hard she tried to be human, she would never think like one.

Her soul had no beginning, middle, or end, she was immortal. For her protection, death was something she accepted. It was all around her.

The dream of living a normal life could never be. Her life died the day she took the blood oath and bowed before the fae queen.

Yet, her heart ached for Kendrick. She felt his pain and how much he missed his wife. She understood firsthand what it had done to this family. If only she could take his pain away.

"If the gods had mercy, I'd ask to trade in all my tomorrows for just one yesterday. I'd show her the husband she deserved."

Leana put her hand on his shoulder. It was the only thing she could do to comfort him, for there were no words to ease his pain.

To her surprise, Kendrick placed his hand on top of hers and squeezed.

"Have ye ever loved someone so much it hurts?" Kendrick gazed at her.

The anguish in his eyes tore at her heart "I've never experienced a love that strong."

"I'd die for her."

Suffering radiated from his body. Leana couldn't bear to see him trapped inside this emotional torture chamber. She had to take his pain away. Not knowing what kind of magic she'd felt in Kendrick, she was taking a huge risk. But she had to do something. No one deserved this amount of cruelty. Looking deep into his brown eyes, Leana caressed his cheek as she absorbed some of his pain. "What was her name?"

"Adamina," his voice cracked.

"'Tis a beautiful name."

"Aye,"

Leana prayed her charm was working. "Tell me what ye remember the most about Adamina."

The corners of his mouth rose. "Her cooking."

"What did she cook for ye?"

"Roasted grouse." She watched him fall deeper under her spell. "I remember how she used to fuss while plucking the feathers. I'd tell her my job was to provide the meat, hers to clean and cook it." He chuckled.

"How did it make ye feel to provide for yer family?"

His smile faded. Shite, did he see through her charm?

Suddenly, his hands were on her hips, pulling her close. "Like a man."

Leana placed her hands on his chest. Instantly, warmth traveled up her arms, causing her to lose focus. Aye, he was much more than a mortal man.

As she probed deeper into his mind and heart, she found the deepest, strongest feelings for Adamina. It wasn't easy, Kendrick hadn't loved freely. But she absorbed the love. The power was unlike anything she'd ever known. He adored his wife.

Was this what true love felt like?

She didn't want to stop the rush of ecstasy, but she knew what she was feeling was not made for her. Stepping into his embrace, Leana wrapped her arms around him and laid her head on his chest, listening to his heartbeat. She squeezed him and poured all of Adamina's love back into him. Where her body touched his, he'd feel that love.

He engulfed her with his big body. All the years of pent-up heartache flowed out of him. Tears rolled down his cheeks as he buried his head against her neck.

"That's it, take her love and live again." She took away years of suffering and replaced it with love and happiness. Even if it wasn't with her, Kendrick's family deserved joy.

"I dinnae know what is happening to me," he whispered in her ear. "I feel weightless, as if the veil of misery has been lifted."

Leana wrapped her arms around his neck, bring his forehead to hers. "Kendrick, know this. Yer love for Adamina will live on. Her death is not the greatest loss in yer life. 'Tis what has died inside ye over the years yer family mourns."

"I...I love her so much. I dinnae know how to let her go."

"Shh." She closed her eyes and caressed the back of his neck, absorbing the rest of the pain. "Dinnae think, Kendrick, just feel me."

9

KENDRICK AWOKE INSIDE HIS BEDCHAMBER. But how in the devil had he ended up undressed and in bed?

He sat up and scrubbed his face, expecting to feel hungover. He'd drank himself into oblivion. But his head didn't throb, nor did the taste of sour ale linger in his mouth.

He scanned his bedchamber, noticing the fire and a tray of food on the table. Davina was curled up in a chair asleep.

What had made him feel like he was at peace? The fog had lifted from his mind and he could think clearly. That hadn't been possible in so many years. He'd spent every day drunk. But now...his body felt alive, like he'd made love all night, and he wanted more.

Shite. Why couldn't he remember who had made him feel this way? He'd been at the shop. Kendrick closed his eyes, remembering more. Adamina's grave... He'd been there with Davina.

Kendrick's eyes shot open. What had he done? He stared at Davina. If he had taken her to bed, she would still be lying next to him. Relief washed over him. Nay, he hadn't made love with her. No amount of ale could make him forget that!

Perplexed, Kendrick laid back down. He kept watch over Davina as he untangled his thoughts. In his condition last night, there'd have been no way to make it back to the keep without help. Davina couldn't have brought him here on her own. He was a big man, too heavy for her to carry.

What had taken place last night?

Kendrick's attention returned to Davina, her perfect lips, dark eyelashes, and flawless skin. He'd never seen a more beautiful woman.

His gaze drifted to her full breasts and her veil of long, curly red hair. He sighed, for he'd felt her softness against him. Aye, he'd touch her again...when the time was right.

Davina stirred. Her dress slipped up her leg, exposing her thigh. He swallowed hard as he imagined trailing kisses up her leg. He bet she tasted sweet like warm honey. The lass had no idea what she had turned him into. Or did she? Did she know he was watching her?

"Ye're awake, my lord."

Kendrick's heart raced as he looked up at her. He felt like a fool getting caught staring. Even if he were free to love, Davina deserved better. "Aye." He sat up, pulling the furs over his lap, hiding his arousal.

His eyes followed the sway of her hips as she walked across the room to a table and poured water into a tankard. She glanced over her shoulder as she tucked a stray hair behind her ear. Her wicked smile said it all as she stared at his cock. She knew how aroused he was and liked it! He licked his lips. For fuck's sake, what did she think of him? "I'm sorry. 'Tis inappropriate."

"I disagree, 'tis verra appropriate." Davina handed him the tankard and sat on the bed.

By the gods, she was so close. All he had to do was lean in and take her in his arms.

Damn him for a fool, he leaned toward her. Aye, she smelled divine. His heart raced as she caressed his forehead. Before he did something stupid, he turned away.

"Ye should know by now I dinnae bite," Leana said. "I need to check for fever."

He grabbed her hand. "It has been a long time since I've had a beautiful woman in me chamber. Forgive me if I seem uneasy."

She gazed into his eyes. "Ye think I'm beautiful?"

"Ye know ye're a bonny lass."

"Hearing it from ye means something special."

"Aye?"

She averted her gaze, but Kendrick lifted her chin, bringing her eyes to his again. "Tell me."

"It does no' matter. Ye've made it perfectly clear ye dinnae want a wife, and I will no' settle for anything less than a husband and family."

"Davina—"

"Nay. I will leave ye to rest." Davina began to leave, but Kendrick stopped her.

"I dinnae want ye to go." He pulled her back down on the bed. "I dinnae know what happened between us at the grave, and dinnae think I want to know. Whatever it was, me head has never been clearer. I feel alive again because of ye. Ye're the light I needed in me dark world." He took her hands in his. "Davina, please do me the honor of being me wife."

Kendrick waited for her response. He couldn't believe how freely the truth had poured out. Giving up the ghost never felt so good. Adamina would want him to be happy; she'd want her children to be happy. Davina had shown him she was the woman his children needed...the woman he needed.

"Kendrick, I dinnae know what to say."

"'Tis want ye want, isn't it?"

"I do. Verra much."

"Then marry me." He cradled her face and stared into her eyes. "There's no denying it, there's a passion between us waiting to be explored. I can feel it. Can ye?"

"God's bones, I felt it the day we first met."

He brushed his lips against hers, taking in their softness. Her breath quickened as he moved his hands down her back. He pulled her close. "I need ye, Davina."

"What are ye waiting for?" She met his lust-filled gaze. "Kiss me."

Kendrick slipped his hand behind her neck, bringing her lips to his. Their tongues dueled in a heated rush. Why had he waited so long to kiss her like this?

"Kendrick," she moaned.

"Lass," he growled. "I love the way me name sounds coming from yer lips." His ears weren't the only thing that loved her moans. His cock ached to be buried deep inside her. It had been a long time. He'd finish before they even got started.

"Kendrick." She placed her hands on his chest and drew away from him. "There's something I must tell ye."

The bedchamber door flew open and Anna strode in, panicked. In shock, she looked at Davina who was wiping her mouth with the back of her hand, then at Kendrick. "Da," she exclaimed.

"Anna," he warned. But as he looked at her, there was something very wrong and it had nothing to do with Davina. "Is it Allie?"

"Nay...I...MacTavish..." She couldn't speak clearly.

Davina walked over to Anna and placed her hands on her shoulders, trying to calm her down. "Slow down lass."

"Davina, something is verra wrong with MacTavish. He's sick."

"MacTavish?" Kendrick roared as he donned his tunic.

"Da, I'm sorry. He needs yer help," Anna pleaded.

"I told ye to stay away from him." He turned to Davina. "Did ye know she was out with the lad?"

"Kendrick, this is no' the time to be scolding yer daughter." Davina turned to Anna. "I can help. Where's the lad?"

10

LEANA FOLLOWED Anna out of the keep to where a black horse waited. Anna mounted, then helped Leana climb up behind her. They reached a thatched-roofed cottage. The stench of rotting flesh filled the air, and Leana dismounted. She could hear the sick lad moaning from inside the hut.

Leana opened the door, sensing death all around her. MacTavish was sprawled out on a pallet covered in sweat and writhing in pain. He was dying. As were his parents, who were on cots next to MacTavish and covered in black blisters, their skin ashen.

"Can ye help him?" Anna stepped inside, a cloth held across her nose and mouth.

"Anna, go home."

"Nay, I will no' leave him. He needs me."

"Anna," Leana warned. "I can no allow ye inside this house. Death will claim everyone here. Ye're no' safe."

"What about ye?"

"By the mercy of the gods, I'll be well. Please, Anna, go."

Tears streamed down the lass's face as she turned and ran out of the house.

Leana knelt next to the lad and felt his forehead. He was on fire.

"Please, help me," he whispered. "I tried to save mum and da. I was too late. One day they were well, dead the next."

Leana had heard tales of the Black Death spreading in shipyards, but never seen it this far inland. It ravaged peoples' bodies without mercy. And the lad had only moments to live.

Leana sat back on her heels. Should she risk everything she'd worked so hard for to heal the boy? The answer came without hesitation. Aye, Anna loved him. Though she'd disobeyed her father to be with him, Leana understood forbidden love. If MacTavish were Kendrick, she'd do anything to save him.

"Today the gods have showed ye mercy. I can help ye." Leana bit into the skin on her wrist, then offered her blood to the lad. 'Drink." Blood dripped into his mouth.

Within seconds, he grew hungrier, latching onto her arm and pulling it closer, sucking her blood. The more he drank, the stronger he got.

"Davina!"

By the gods, what was Kendrick doing there? She yanked her arm away from MacTavish.

Kendrick entered the cottage. "Are ye hurt?"

"Nay, but ye must leave."

"I won't leave ye here alone. What can I do to help?'

Leana looked up at him. "Check the rest of tenants. Bring me the sick and burn the dead."

"Aye."

Kendrick lifted MacTavish's mother from her pallet.

"Wait." Leana ripped a strip of material from the hem of

her gown. "Cover yer nose and mouth to keep death from entering yer body."

He put the body down and did as Davina had instructed.

"Kendrick, whatever ye do, dinnae look into the eyes of the dead."

Kendrick nodded.

Hours later, twenty sick men, women, and children filled the cottage, all laid out on makeshift pallets. There was no room to walk. Secretly, Leana had fed them her blood until they were on the mend, resting peacefully. She'd found some sage and cleansed the house of all evil. She'd washed their skin with rosewater to chase death from their bodies. She'd even used her power to absorb their pain. By doing so much for them, she'd left herself vulnerable and weak. She hadn't fed in a long time, but was strong enough to heal these people.

What had compelled her to save these families? Her love for Anna? Or was it to redeem herself from taking Davina's life? She knew she was toying with destiny, and not even a blood drinker had the right to interfere with fate. Whatever the truth, helping the sick made her feel needed. Healing a mother so she could hold her child again, or a man so he could hold the woman he loved, made the risk to her own wellbeing worth it.

A woman coughed as she struggled to get Leana's attention. "Thank ye for helping us."

Leana smiled as she knelt and held the woman's hand. "What do ye mean?"

"Ye came for our souls. But ye chose mercy instead."

How could a human possibly know that?

"Ye're the Angel of Death."

Leana laughed. "If I were the Angel of Death, ye'd be dead."

"Ye offered yer blood to all of us. Ye healed us."

Leana knew what she had to do—charm the woman into believing another story. "What ye witnessed was a miracle from yer god. Not from me."

The woman nodded as she struggled to keep her eyes open. She laid the woman's hand on her chest, then tucked the blanket around her.

Relief washed over Leana as she stood—the woman wouldn't remember. But what if someone else had seen her offer her blood to the dying? She prayed the others wouldn't remember her as the Angel of Death.

She couldn't erase their memories, then they'd completely forget her, and that would raise suspicion with Kendrick and Anna who knew she was there.

Suddenly, the room began to spin and Leana couldn't breathe. She needed air.

A blast of cold air hit her as she stumbled outside gasping for air. It was happening all over again. When would she learn to accept life for what it was? She had no right to change their fate. Because of her poor judgment, she could end up dead.

Ye saved these people out of love.

Conflicted, Leana staggered to a nearby tree and sat. So many thoughts raged inside her. It had felt right to help Kendrick's tenants, especially MacTavish. But in doing so, she'd sacrificed her own life. All she could do was pray that the old woman would stay silent.

Why must I tempt fate?

A blood drinker didn't belong in this realm. She was a monster for taking Davina's life and the two lads from the blacksmith shop. Everywhere she went, death followed.

Burning flesh filled her senses. Leana pulled herself up and followed the smell. Ash mixed with snow flurried around Kendrick as he burned the last body. Lines etched his face, shattering her heart. She couldn't imagine the loss he was feeling. His tenants were like family.

She prayed the suffering was over.

Kendrick met Leana's gaze. She was tired and didn't know what to say or do to ease his pain. Holding back a flood of tears, Leana took a deep breath. Her mouth opened but nothing came out.

In long purposeful strides, Kendrick approached, pulling down the cloth covering his mouth. He took her head in his hands. "Are ye well, lass?"

She nodded, and Kendrick tugged her into his arms. The warmth of his touch chased away all of Leana's fears. He squeezed her tight as she wrapped her arms around him, burying her head against his neck. She couldn't hold in the tears anymore.

"I'm taking ye home, Davina." Kendrick picked her up, cradling her in his arms. "I'm going to take care of ye," he whispered.

Davina? She wanted to tell him she was a fraud—she didn't deserve to live Davina's life anymore. With her body withered in exhaustion, she laid her head against his chest, ready to tell him the truth. She opened her mouth, then shut it. *Nay.* She took in his warmth. She couldn't let him go —not tonight.

11

KENDRICK PACED outside his chamber where Davina slept. Knowing what had happened the last time they were alone made him nervous. He wanted her. Each time he checked on her, his resolve broke a little more. The desire to slip in bed and hold her proved to be more than he could handle.

What are ye waiting for, eejit?

Taking a deep breath, he opened the door. He peeked at the bed but Davina wasn't there. "Davina," he called.

"Aye."

He walked in. "How are ye?" Davina was in the tub.

"I'm well, thank ye."

He averted his gaze. "I'm sorry. I didnae know ye were…"

"Naked?"

"Aye." He raked his fingers through his hair. "I'll come back later."

"Stay."

Kendrick walked closer as he rubbed the tension from the back of his neck. "Ye look well."

"A wee bit of sleep and a hot bath does the body good. It was nice of Anna to draw me a bath."

"Anna did this?"

"Aye. I think she's beginning to like me." She smiled.

"I'm sorry for accusing ye of knowing about Anna sneaking off with the MacTavish lad."

"Kendrick, I did know."

"What?"

"Please dinnae be mad. Anna told me where she was going. I talked to her about the lad, love, and the consequences of her actions. She's a smart lass. Ye need to trust her."

"'Tis no' her I dinnae trust."

"I know. But mayhap if ye let her make her own decisions, yer relationship with her will be better. I can assure ye, there is no lad that comes before her da. She loves ye."

Kendrick should be mad at Davina for betraying his trust, but he couldn't be. She was right. Anna had been rebelling against his rules because, truthfully, he'd been an arse. Anna was old enough to make her own decisions even though they might not be what he wanted for her.

Kendrick pulled up a chair and sat next to the tub. "I dinnae know when it happened, but me first born has grown up right before me eyes and I was too blind to see it."

"Ye're a good father." Davina placed her wet hand on his thigh. "Ye are allowed to make mistakes. She forgives ye. She misses her mother."

"Aye." He exhaled heavily. "'Tis time for a new beginning." He glanced at Davina, and she gave him a warm smile.

"I'm glad ye finally realize that."

"Thanks to ye, Davina." Their gazes locked.

Mutual hunger pulled them closer together. Her wet hair clung to her pale skin, and the fire in the hearth cast a soft glow over her body. By the saints, he wanted the lass.

"Do ye want to join me, Kendrick?" She pinned him with a wicked grin that she knew he couldn't resist.

He stared at her full lips and couldn't deny himself any longer. He stood and removed his tunic. He unlaced his trews, allowing them to fall to floor. Her gaze heated his body as she looked him up and down, approving of his masculine physique.

She licked her lips. "From the first day I met ye, I imagined how ye'd look naked."

"Och, lass, do I meet yer expectations?"

"Oh, aye." She winked.

Kendrick stepped inside the tub. The warm water and the smell of roses soothed his body as he sat down in front of Davina. "I have a confession of me own."

"Ye do?" She handed him a wet cloth, then turned so her back faced him. She pulled her hair over her shoulder.

"I've dreamt many times of making love to ye." He rubbed the cloth across her back.

Slowly, she turned around. It was hard to read her thoughts. Did she want him in that way? Had he overstepped his boundaries again? He prayed not. "Davina, I'm sorry. I didnae mean to make ye feel uncomfortable. I should leave."

Feeling like a fool, he began to stand. Davina grabbed his hand and pulled him back down into the water. "Ye are a daft man, Kendrick the Fletcher. If I didnae want things between us to go further than friendship, I would no' have asked ye to get naked and share a bath with me."

Kendrick chuckled. "Ye're right. 'Tis been a long time."

Davina moved closer, straddling his lap. She rose from the water and cupped his face. "I think ye know I want ye.

We have all night." She dipped her head down and claimed his lips.

Wanting to taste more, he plunged his tongue in her mouth, deepening the kiss. He pulled her onto his lap. As if he wasn't hard enough from seeing her naked, her wet, hot heat brushed against his cock. "God's bones, Davina," he moaned against her neck. "Ye set me on fire."

"'Tis a good thing we're sitting in water."

"No amount of water can extinguish these flames." He trailed kisses down her neck. The lass was quickly sending him over the edge. By tasting every delectable inch of her, it grew harder to resist.

He cupped her breasts, admiring their perfection. "Ye're verra beautiful." He dipped his head and claimed a nipple in his mouth.

"Kendrick," she reached between them and wrapped her hand around his cock. "Make love to me," she whispered in his ear.

With one thrust, he buried himself deep inside. White light flickered behind his eyes and his body came to life, as if every nerve ending ignited all at once. "Incredible."

"I never felt anything like it. Do it again."

He cupped her arse with both hands and guided her up and down his cock. Water sloshed, spilling over the tub. It was like some primal beast had taken him over. *Davina*. All he could think about was her. The way she felt, hot and wet. Her soft breasts pressed against his chest. The taste of her salty skin...

Her body stiffened as he pumped into her harder and faster. Aye, he liked it like that, how she threw her head back in ecstasy, the way she clawed at his hands as pleasure overtook them both. Her lips parted and she moaned his name. Nothing was sweeter than hearing his name coming for her mouth.

She trembled as he watched her shatter right before him. His own body begged for release. He cupped her face. "Look at me."

She met his eyes, and that's all it took—he came so hard it shook him to the core.

She melted against his chest, and he held her close, kissing the top of her head. "Was this as good as yer dream?" she asked.

"Davina, ye are what good dreams are made of. However, good does no' come close to describing how I'm feeling right now."

"So." She sat up. "I've pleased ye?" She smiled wickedly.

"Och, lass, beyond." He winked as he took her hand and brought it to his lips. Her fingertips where wrinkled from soaking in the water so long. "I think we should get dry and warm before we catch our deaths."

She smiled. "Aye, however I can no' stand. "Ye've left me boneless."

"I can help." Kendrick pulled her into his arms and stood. "Once yer ready, I want to love ye properly."

"Kendrick, if what ye just did to me wasn't proper, then I must be in for a treat."

"Och, lass, I'm just getting started."

"Who are ye?" Leana whispered as she traced Kendrick's jawline with her finger while he slept. A tingle spread across her stomach as she recalled the roughness of that stubble against her inner thighs. What he'd done with his tongue had rendered her speechless.

There was no denying it; some kind of magic had happened between them. As if they were destined to be together.

She took in the hard lines of his face. Sorrow filled her, for she knew the story behind those lines. Leaning in, she placed a soft kiss on his parted lips. "I love ye, Kendrick the Fletcher."

His dark eyelashes rested on his cheeks, reminding her of a mighty raven's wing. He was her undoing.

It surprised her how heavy her lies weighed on her heart. "Ye deserve better." She threaded her fingers through his long, sorrel hair. Beyond being attracted to him, Kendrick had changed her. She no longer wanted to hide her true self. She wanted him to know everything about her, but how could she tell him? It would cost her everything.

Carefully, she climbed out of bed and dressed. Before she could open her heart to Kendrick, there was one person she had to make peace with.

Leana rode her horse through the thick snow blanketing the forest. There was little time to waste before morn broke. Kendrick would be up and wondering where she'd gone. Leana leaned over her horse's neck and said, "God speed, beastie."

A clearing not far from the tavern came into view. Giving the reins a tug, Leana halted and dismounted next to a rowan tree. The berries glowed red against the snow collecting on its branches. Leana took in the glory of winter. Flurries floated to the ground in an enchanting dance. The air was cold and crisp and burned her lungs whenever she took a deep breath.

She knelt in front of Davina's shallow grave. An image flashed through her mind, the lass staring up at her from her resting place. She hadn't suffered. Leana laid her to rest peacefully, but that didn't make it right. It was wrong to take Davina's life, but most of all, to trick her.

She could have saved Davina, but hadn't. All because of her own selfish desire to live as a human again.

She'd tried to change her fate before and look where that landed her. Forever beautiful...forever a blood drinker... forever *Baobhan sith*.

Even blood drinkers had to obey fate. Life was such a fragile thing; she'd taken Davina's without a care.

The only way to make amends with Davina was for Leana to purify her soul by becoming who she was meant to be. No more lies, no false hopes about being human.

"Davina, I took something precious from ye. I could have healed ye." Leana swallowed back tears. "I'd say I'm sorry, but deep down, I'm no'. If it wasn't for ye, I would no' be standing here a changed woman. Ye made me see life is precious. I believe the gods brought us together. Ye must think I'm mad. I'm dammed and do no' deserve the gods' mercy nor yer forgiveness. So, I will no' ask ye to forgive me. Just know, ye were the angel who saved me."

Tears streamed down Leana's cheeks and fell onto the grave. She covered her face with both hands and wept. A warm sensation spread across her skin. The scent of heather and bog myrtle wafted through the air. Leana looked up. "Davina?"

Even though she couldn't see her, Leana felt Davina's embrace. It gave her comfort knowing Davina had forgiven her.

"Thank ye, lass," Leana whispered.

12

ADAIRA, Masie, and Kerr rode through the forest desperately trying to catch up with Rafe and Tegwyn. But once the wolves caught Leana's scent, there was no holding them back. Adaira pushed her horse as far as the beast could run without causing injury.

She rounded the bend and there stood Rafe naked from the shift.

"What took you so long?"

It always amazed her how powerful and stunning Rafe's wolf was. But seeing him naked was more rewarding.

"Ye fancy what ye see, my queen?" Rafe sauntered over to Adaira.

Grinning like the devil, she threw his clothes at him. "Ye better dress quickly before Masie sees ye in all yer naked glory."

Adaira dismounted, and before her feet hit the ground, Rafe tugged her into his arms. "How much time do we have until they catch up?" Rafe waggled his dark brows.

As much as Adaira wanted him, this wasn't the time or place for a quick romp. She had to find Leana. "Rafe." She shook her head. "Put yer clothes on. We dinnae have time for this."

"I know, my queen." He kissed her neck. "There's something different about ye that's driving me wild."

"I dinnae know what ye mean. Nothing has changed."

Rafe paused and looked at her. He placed his hands on her stomach. "Are ye—"

"Nay. Are ye daft? I'm no' with child." Adaira pushed him away. "A wolf and blood drinker can no' have children together."

"Are ye sure? Ye cannot trick a wolf's keen senses. Besides, how do ye know for sure we cannot have children? 'Tis not like we have another wolf and *Baobhan sith* couple to compare us with. Have ye been ill? Unusually tired? Ravenous with hunger?"

Adaira paused for a moment. Aye, she'd craved blood more than usual. And she couldn't get enough of the cook's oatcakes lately. She normally hated them. But to say she was with child because she was hungry was nonsense. "Rafe Madok, yer daft to think me with child." She climbed on her horse.

As Rafe dressed, Adaira placed her hand on her stomach. Could she be with child? She was sick every morn —she could sleep for days—and the fact that Rafe sensed it...

The sound of horse hooves thundering made Adaira look over her shoulder.

Masie and Kerr had finally caught up.

"Why have we stopped. Is Leana near?" Masie asked Kerr.

"Aye," Tegwyn said. "Just past the wood fence there's a keep. That's where she's staying."

"What are we waiting for?" Kerr asked. "Let's go."

"Nay," Masie said. "Adaira and I will go alone."

"I do no' like this plan, Masie. Ye're with child. We dinnae know who else is in the keep. 'Tis too dangerous."

"Kerr," Masie argued, "Adaira and I *must* go alone. We can no' risk frightening Leana."

"I will no' allow Masie to be harmed. Dinnae underestimate our power," Adaira said.

Kerr shook his head.

"We'll make camp and wait for yer return," Rafe said. "Be careful."

Adaira smiled at her wolf. "Aye."

Adaira and Maisie rode off.

"They'll be watching our every move." Adaira said with a grin.

"Aye, sister, they are a stubborn lot. As long as they stay hidden, I dinnae care. Kerr has seen me beast, and I'm no' afraid to free her from her cage if I have to."

"Let's pray it does no' come to that."

Once they reached the keep, they dismounted and Adaira marched up the steps and knocked on the door. But Masie stopped her.

Adaira's brows creased in irritation. "What the devil, Masie?"

"Wait. There's something odd here. Do ye feel it?"

Adaira took a step back and gently placed her hand on the door. A tingling sensation traveled up her arm and raced through her veins. Her heart slammed into her ribcage. She turned to Masie with wide eyes. "Magic."

"Aye. Tread softly," Masie whispered. "We dinnae know who or what is in there."

Fear streaked down her spine. What if Leana was being held there against her will? Mayhap she tried to escape and couldn't. What if the queen had found her first? Adaira knocked on the door again. "Maiden, Mother, Crone," she whispered as she waited for someone to answer. She turned to Masie. "Remind me to never take me eyes off Leana again."

Kendrick rushed downstairs and into the kitchen expecting to find Davina. Waking up alone wasn't the way he wanted to start the day. The taste of her still lingered on his tongue, and he craved more. "Davina," he called as he rounded the corner. "What the devil?"

Finn looked up from stuffing his mouth full of bread. "She's no' here."

"What are ye doing in me house?"

Finn swallowed a mouthful of mead. "I thought to fill me belly before Kit and I go into town for supplies."

"Dinnae ye have food at yer house?"

"Nay, I dinnae have a bonny lass to feed me like ye do." Finn grinned as he shoved a hunk of bread into his mouth. "Have ye lost her already?"

"Nay," Kendrick grumbled. "She's here. Mayhap with Allie."

Finn shook his head. "Anna left with Allie over an hour ago."

"Did Anna say where they were going?"

"Nay."

"God's bones." Kendrick shoved his hand through his hair in frustration. "Why can no' anyone tell me where they are going?

Finn shrugged and popped another piece of bread into his mouth.

A knock at the door sound. With the plague wiping out more than half of the tenants, who could be at the door?

Kendrick opened it and found two beautiful women. "Can I help? Are ye lost?"

"Nay, we are no' lost," the fair-haired lass spoke up. "May we come in?"

Compelled by their beauty, he let them in.

"Thank ye," she said as she walked past.

Kendrick shut the door and turned around, meeting the fair-haired woman's hand.

"I'm Masie Keith Gunn and this is me sister Adaira Keith."

He shook her hand. "Kendrick Fletcher."

"Our sister is missing," Adaira said. "We believe she's here."

"Please, come in." Kendrick motioned for the women to sit down at the gathering table. Dread washed over him. What if one of the many who succumbed to the sickness was their missing sister. *Dear god, have mercy.* "When was the last time ye saw her?"

"Over three months ago," Masie said.

"What did she look like?"

"She's as tall as me," Adaira said. "Slender."

Tall and slender. With that description, it could have been one of the woman he'd buried. Mayhap Finn remembered the lass. "Finn?"

"Aye." Finn rounded the corner and froze.

"This is Masie and Adaira. They are looking for their missing sister. Mayhap ye have seen her."

Apparently, Finn too was bewitched by their beauty to speak. "Finn," Kendrick exclaimed.

"Aye..." Finn answered. "What does she look like."

"Tall and slender," Kendrick answered.

Finn sat down at the table next to Masie. "Hello." He winked.

Masie grinned. "Finn, have ye seen our sister?"

"I'm sorry." Kendrick interrupted Finn, saving him from further humiliation. "Plague has put many of me people in the grave recently..."

"The sickness would no' affect her." Masie said. "Please, think harder. She has fire-red hair. 'Tis long like mine, but curly."

"She has blue eyes," Adaira added.

Kendrick sat back. Red hair, blue eyes, and slender?

"Och, I've seen her," Finn exclaimed. "Kendrick, ye swine, ye've been keeping these beauties a secret. Davina, has sisters?" He smiled at Masie. "By the saints, today is a good day."

"Davina?" Adaira questioned. "Nay, her name is—"

Suddenly, the door swung open and in rushed Davina. "Kendrick, we need to talk."

Kendrick stood from the table. "Aye, we do."

Kendrick watched her as she looked shocked to see the women sitting at the table.

"Leana," Masie exclaimed as she ran to her sister. "I thought we'd lost ye forever."

"How did ye find me?"

Adaira rose from the table. "Tegwyn and Bhaltair tracked ye here."

"So, 'tis true." Kendrick said with furrowed brows. "They are yer sisters?" As he approached her, she stepped back. "Ye told me yer family died during a house fire. Why didnae ye tell me the truth, Davina?"

"Here name is Leana," Adaira said. "What lies have ye brought here?"

"Lies? There's more than one?" Kendrick continued

walking toward her until he pinned her against the wall. "Tell me, lass, is it true? Is yer name Leana and are these women yer sisters?"

"Aye, I wanted to tell ye."

"Leana." Adaira strode to her sister. "He does no' know, does he?"

Kendrick's blood boiled with anger, his eyes narrowing on her. "Know what?"

"Please," Leana pleaded. "I can explain everything."

"Nay." Adaira grabbed Leana's arm, pulling her away from the wall. "Ye have done enough here. Ye are coming with us to Dornoch."

Leana pulled away. "Dornoch? Have ye gone mad? Have ye forgotten I'm wanted for murder?"

"Murder?" Kendrick exclaimed.

"Nay, Leana," Masie joined them. "Ye didnae kill those laddies. The dark prince did. Adaira saw everything."

"What?" Leana said, dumfounded.

"'Tis true," Adaira confirmed.

"Cormag is dead, and Adaira is now the laird of Dornoch. Ye can come home now," Masie said.

"I dinnae understand." Leana walked over to the table and sat down.

Masie joined her, putting her arm around her sister. "I've missed ye. We have so much to talk about. Please, Leana come home."

"Ye can no' stay here," Adaira said. "Ye're in danger. We all are."

"The queen," Leana whispered.

"Aye." Adaira placed her hand on Leana's shoulder. "If ye care about these people, ye'll leave now."

"Aye, I think 'tis best ye all leave." Kendrick opened the door.

Leana stood and slowly walked toward him. He couldn't look at her. What an eejit, he'd fallen in love with a liar. Who was this woman? Did he even care? She'd shattered his heart, but most of all, she'd betrayed his trust.

"Please, let me explain. I'll tell ye everything."

Kendrick's head was spinning with anger. Furious with himself for allowing her into his home and trusting her with his children, he averted his gaze. He was done being the fool.

"Look at me, Kendrick."

He refused to give in to her pleading.

"I can explain. I meant ye no harm."

Damn the devil, he looked at her and fell into her wicked trap. He closed the door. Was he really going to listen to what she had to say? *Shite.* He grabbed her arm, pulling her toward the kitchen so they could be alone. Could he trust her enough to tell the truth? Regardless, he'd never play the fool again.

13

LEANA'S SCENT had drawn the dark prince to a shallow grave. He took a deep breath, holding back the rage brewing inside. *She can't be dead.* His fell to his knees next to the mound. *No!*

He cursed himself for not finding Leana sooner. However, she hadn't make it easy. Leaving no trail, she'd covered her tracks masterfully. He'd taught her well.

The winter wind blew cold against Alder's skin, ruffling his black wings as he hung his head, mourning his beloved Leana. The agonizing pain in his chest felt as if it'd been sliced open by a hundred daggers.

It was true, she'd bewitched him the first day he set eyes on her in the forest ten years ago. He'd watched her grow into a beautiful woman. He'd been patient when she refused him. Why not, he had forever to convince the lass to love him. He loved seeing her spread her wings and fly, as long as he was there to catch her when she fell.

Forever was gone now. He'd been too patient. Why did he allow her to leave the Unseelie realm?

Ever since Leana had escaped the fae realm, he'd

watched over her and even killed for her. He could have brought her to the queen many times—but didn't. That was his first mistake.

Ah yes, the humans at the blacksmith shop. Until that night, he'd never felt blood burning hatred before. Seeing Leana with two men sparked jealousy inside him. Looking back, he wished he could have blamed his actions on losing his self-control, but the truth was he was very aware of what he was doing. He enjoyed ripping through those bastard's flesh.

Leana had seen the beast he'd become. He saw the terror in her eyes as she watched him kill. He invited her to watch. However, he'd pushed her too far. She was beyond terrified of him. All hope of bringing her home had been lost, so he'd scrubbed her mind of everything that happened that night and left her in the shop.

Alder pounded his fist into the ground. Why did he allow this? He'd let her get out of control, and now she was dead. It was his fault. He should have protected her.

A wave of despair washed over him. Through tear-filled eyes, he looked at the grave. Clumps of tiny green stems broke through the snow. He cocked his head to the side as he watched the stems grow long, skinny leaves. At the top, pale green bubs unfolded into white petals shaped like bells that drooped.

"Snowdrop," he whispered. Leana couldn't be dead. Only the tears from a *Baobhan sith* created by the snow queen produced snowdrop flowers. Alder stood. There was hope. If Leana wasn't buried in the grave, who was? What had this person meant to Leana to make her cry? A tinge of jealousy pricked up his spine as he thought of it being another man.

Alder glared at the unmarked grave and with a blink,

caused the flowers to wilt. He breathed in the cold forest air and through the pungent spicy smell of pine trees her sweet scent lingered. "Dearest Goddess," he exclaimed.

"It won't be long now, my wildflower. I will find you."

Alder stood and stretched his massive black wings. He pumped them twice and ascended above the forest, clearing the tall pines. Leana's scent floated in the air, awakening all his senses. He soared out of sight.

Her sweetness led him to a keep beyond the hillside. As silent as a whisper, Alder landed on the roof. He crouched on the ledge of the battlements, studying his surroundings below. Although the warrior inside him urged to storm through the door and take back what was his, he had to strike when the time was right.

The wind ruffled his feathers bringing another scent to his attention. *Masie and Adaira.*

What were they doing here?

He stood, knowing he should notify the queen. Her majesty would be pleased. Alder unfolded his wings, ready to take flight back to the fae realm, but stopped. He faced the wind and honed into a voice. *Leana.*

Without hesitation, he scrubbed all thoughts of returning to the queen. He needed to see Leana.

From the outside he'd seen two ways to enter the keep— one, the front great hall door and two, the kitchen door. Both not the ideal way in, but he had no choice. He was sure there were hidden tunnels and passage ways leading in, but where to look he didn't know.

But what he did know was Leana's voice, and it would lead him to her.

He jumped off the ledge and flew behind the keep to the kitchen. It was risky, but he had no choice.

He approached the kitchen door and crept inside. He

drew his dagger ready to strike, but to his surprise no one was here. He made his way across the kitchen when he heard footsteps. He dashed behind a whiskey barrel.

Someone strode into the kitchen. He chanced taking a glance from behind the barrel, for the footsteps were too heavy to be Leana's. The air in his lungs seized. *Leana.*

She was as beautiful as ever with a wild tangle of red curls and pink cheeks. Had someone upset her? She wasn't alone. A brawny man held her arm, pulling her into the kitchen. A low, gurgling growl vibrated up Alder's throat. He moved into attack stance, ready to kill, but stopped himself after the man started to speak.

"Davina...Leana, whoever ye are, ye have a lot of explaining to do. What kind of evil have ye brought into me home?"

Alder relaxed. What had Leana be up to?

"Kendrick, if ye'll calm down, I'll tell ye everything."

"No lies."

"Aye," Leana agreed.

"I'm listening." Kendrick folded his arms across his chest.

"I dinnae know where to start. I've told so many lies me head is spinning." Leana wrung her hands together.

"How about ye start by telling me who or what ye are."

"Not yer kind."

"'Och, lass, that is painfully obvious from what I've heard from yer sisters. Murder, a dark prince, and a fae queen—"

"Kendrick, I'm a blood drinker, a *Baobhan sith*."

The room grew cold and silent. Even Alder could feel the uncomfortable tension.

"Please, say something," Leana begged.

There was a long pause before Kendrick answered. "I have no words."

Leana took a step closer to Kendrick.

"Ye must believe I'd never hurt ye or the children. I wanted to tell ye, but I didn't think ye'd understand. I tried to forget who I am, but the more time I spent with ye, the more I felt like me. Ye made me want things I never thought I could have, a home, family of me own, and a man I love."

"Ye should have told me."

"I should have told ye what? That I'm a monster?" Leana took in a deep breath. "I wasn't always like this.

"What happened?"

"I had enough of me father's abuse toward me mother. Desperate to put an end to it, I prayed every night for a way to stop him from hurting her. One night, as I looked for a falling star, fairy fire appeared. I followed the fairies into the glen. Adaira warned me not to trust the fae, but I had no other choice. I made a blood oath with the fae queen, and in return, she would make sure me father would never harm us again. It was a trick. My sisters and me were turned into blood drinkers."

"Ye sacrificed yerself to protect yer mother?"

"Aye. Every time I try to protect me family, I make things worse. I wanted to hide so I wouldn't hurt anyone again. That's when I met Davina. I promised to never take an innocent life again. But she was dying, so I stole her identity. And then I met ye."

"Blame Finn. He brought me to the tavern to pick a wife. I wasn't expecting to find one."

Alder's heart ripped in two. He couldn't believe what he was hearing. Leana was his, but she loved Kendrick.

"Kendrick, can ye forgive me?"

"I dinnae know. Ye betrayed me, and that's something I

can no' forgive so easily." Kendrick said. "Damn the devil, lass. I loved ye, and yet, right now, I dinnae know who ye are. Me children loved ye."

"I'm still Davina."

Kendrick stared at Leana. "Do ye know what it feels like to fall in love with someone ye thought ye knew?

"Kendrick, please forgive me."

"I can no'." Kendrick strode out of the kitchen.

Alder watched Leana fall to her knees, weeping.

Though he wanted to comfort her, she deserved the pain. She knew the rules; a blood drinker belonged in the fae world, not this one. It was time she was held accountable for her actions.

Inside, Alder wept for Leana. Not for her broken heart, but for what he had to do now—report back to the queen.

14

WITH HER HEART SHATTERED, Leana walked back into the great hall where her sisters waited. She met Masie's sympathetic gaze, then Adaira's. Leana knew what she'd done was wrong.

"Leana, I'm so sorry," Masie said as she sat next to her at the table.

She turned to Masie. "Sorry?"

"Aye, we heard everything." Adaira claimed the seat on the other side of Leana. "Kendrick said we could stay until morn, but he wants us gone before the children awake."

Leana laughed mirthlessly. "I was excepting him to prepare our nooses."

"Ye can no' mean that," Masie said, shaking her head. "I know yer heart is broken but give Kendrick some time." Masie put her arm around Leana. Maiden, Mother, Crone, how she'd missed her sister's comforting arms. "He's verra handsome."

"Aye, I have never loved someone the way I love him. Och..." She turned to Masie. "I wish ye could meet Anna, Allie, and Kit."

Masie brows furrowed. "Who are they?"

"His children." Desolation washed over her; she'd never see them again.

"'Tis best this all came out now," Adaira added. "We have bigger problems. The queen must be dealt with."

"Aye," Leana agreed. "But how?"

"Adaira has a plan," Masie said.

Adaira always had a plan. A day without a plan was a day with chaos. Leana had heard that saying from Adaira since the day she was born. As much as she hated hearing it, she was thankful.

"We're going to kill the queen," Adaira said.

"Kill the queen?" Leana asked, then quickly covered her mouth as if the queen could hear her. "We dinnae have an army and there's no force powerful enough to fight her and the fae army."

"Och, sister, ye are wrong. Clans Keith and Gunn combined with the Honor Guard will make a worthy threat."

Leana disagreed. "Nay, ye can no' bring innocent men into this fight. I can no' allow it."

"As laird, I can." Adaira stood. "Dinnae ye think I'm aware of the risks?"

"The queen will devour those men like a hungry wolf who hasn't eaten for days."

"Mayhap we dinnae need to fight at all," Masie said nervously looking into her lap. "I've been keeping something from ye. Mother is alive."

Leana and Adaira turned to Masie. "What!"

"Aye. When I left Raven's Landing, the auld woman driving the cart was Mum. She knew we were there."

"Why didnae ye say something?" Leana asked.

"I wasn't sure if she was real or fae trickery. But if she's alive, mayhap she can help."

"Do ye know where to find her?" Adaira asked.

Masie shook her head. "Mayhap she'll come to us."

"We dinnae have time to wait," Adaira said. "We must strike now."

Leana fell silent as her sisters argued. The great hall turned red as Leana thought about the queen killing everyone she loved. Snowdrop knew how to get what she wanted. Her majesty was doing it now by turning them against one another.

Their aunt probably already knew about Kendrick and the children. A chill raced down her back as if the queen was clawing at her. She'd protect Kendrick at all costs. He was right. What kind of evil had she brought into his home? She had to make things right.

Leana walked up the stairs ignoring her sisters. Quite frankly, their constant bickering made her head hurt. They knew where to find a bed if they wished to rest. However, Leana knew there'd be no sleep tonight. Adaira was desperate to battle the queen, and Masie was hell-bent on talking her out of it. War could be avoided if her sisters agreed to follow her plan.

Leana arrived on the floor where the children slept. She stopped outside Allie's chamber and placed her hand on the door. Every night before bed, Leana checked on Allie. She was going to miss the wee lass.

The door creaked open, and Allie was standing there rubbing her tired eyes. "Is it morn yet?" She yawned.

Leana knelt in front of Allie. "No, lassie. Ye should be in bed."

"I can no' sleep. Ye haven't tucked me in."

"Allie, I..." Leana looked into the child's blue eyes. She couldn't tell Allie the truth.

She walked Allie back inside her bedchamber, going against Kendrick's wishes to stay away from his children. "I'll tuck ye in but ye must promise to be a good lass and go to sleep."

Allie climbed into bed. "Will ye lie down with me until I fall asleep?"

Leana sat on the edge of the mattress. "Why do ye want me to stay?" she asked.

"I dreamt ye were gone."

A tear slipped down Leana's cheek as she thought of never seeing Allie again. "Come here, wee one."

Allie threw her arms around her neck. "Promise me ye'll never leave."

She held her tight. "Och, dinnae fash yerself. No matter where ye go, I will follow."

"I love ye, Davina."

Davina. Hearing that name made her heart heavy with guilt. It wasn't her right to tell Allie the truth, but something deep within her felt the need to do something kind.

Leana scooted away from Allie. She took in a deep breath. The wee lass was innocent. When she was Allie's age, Leana witnessed how cruel the world could be. It was the first time she saw her father raise his fist to her mother.

Nay, she could not bring herself to introduce Allie to her wicked world. Knowing how her own heart ached, she couldn't do the same to Allie. Eventually, the lass would find out, but she wouldn't be here to witness the pain.

Leana snuggled close to Allie. She hugged the lass tight

and brushed a lock of red hair from the lass's face and kissed her forehead. "Go to sleep."

Allie smiled and closed her eyes. Leana took in the moment as she ran her fingers through Allie's hair. This beautiful, peaceful moment would be one she'd never forget.

As soon as the sweet lass fell asleep, Leana slipped out of the bed and went to the door. She looked over her shoulder. "Until I see ye again." She blew a kiss, then quit the bedchamber.

Leana crept downstairs. Praying no one was in the great hall, she rounded the corner and her heart plummeted. Kendrick was hunched over with his head resting on the table. Two empty pitchers were overturned. By the smell of the room, the ale had been flowing throughout the night.

She wanted to lift the fool up by his hair and scold him for getting drunk again. He needed her. But she couldn't blame him for rejecting her. She'd confessed to something wicked and couldn't imagine what had gone through his mind.

She knew what must be done, and it was the ultimate sacrifice. The one thing that would right all her wrongs.

"I never meant to hurt ye," she whispered as she stepped closer to him. "I know what I have to do to keep ye and me sisters safe. In time, I pray ye'll forgive me." She bent down and kissed his cheek. "I love ye, Kendrick the fletcher."

With that, she donned her cloak and walked out the door.

Heavy snow had started to fall, and Leana shielded her face with her hands as she trudged through the snow until she was far away from the keep. She spun around, searching for any sign of Alder. "I know ye're here. Ye're always here," Leana exclaimed. "I'm surrendering to the queen."

Silence filled the night air. She turned to the forest. It was still and calm. Why wasn't he answering her? The queen had won.

Behind her, the trees rustled as the dark prince landed. He folded his wings and slowly drifted toward her.

As he came closer Leana could no longer hold back her anger. "Ye left me to take the blame for murder." She swung and punched him in the stomach.

The prince slammed against a tree. Clumps of snow came raining down on his head from the branches above.

"Ye've ruined me life." Leana strode to the prince and raised her hands, ready to blast him with powerful white light. "I will destroy ye just like ye have destroyed me."

Leana called forth the fury storming deep inside her. Like a swirling tempest, all the anger and hurt spiraled up her body. Blinding light shot from her hands, hitting the prince's chest. Tears streamed down her face as she released her wrath. Years of hate for the queen poured out of her, and she wouldn't stop until every last drop of evil left her body and entered Alder.

She glared at Alder in shock, apparently the light didn't hurt him. In a flash, he lifted her off the ground, her toes dangling above the earth. She struggled to free herself, clawing at his icy grip.

"I had to get your attention, stubborn woman," Alder growled.

"I could think of other ways than murder," she said breathlessly.

"Aye, but you pushed me too far." He leaned close. "Jealousy makes a man do wicked things."

Her stomach knotted as his hot breath swept over her skin. "'Tis time ye came home, Leana. You can't run from the queen. Surrender now, and your peasant farmer won't share the same fate as the Keith lads."

Leana gritted her teeth. How did he know about Kendrick?

"I watch your every move, Leana. I heard you confess your love for that human swine. I can give you everything, pleasure you in ways beyond your wildest dreams, but still you find comfort in this rotting world. What does he have that I don't?"

"A heart."

Alder turned his head as if he couldn't believe what she'd said. His brows creased and he pressed his lips together.

"Go on, punish me. That is what you want to do."

"No." He loosened his grip and placed her on the ground. "The last thing I want to do is hurt you."

As soon as Leana's feet hit the ground, she gasped for air.

"Leana, my red-haired beauty, I love you."

His words chilled her to the bone. He loved her? How could a dark prince love anyone?

Alder scooped Leana into his arms, and in one leap, they were in the sky heading toward the Frozen Isles to the winter vale of the fae court.

Somewhere between the mist rising from the isles and the Forest of Destiny, a weightlessness came over Leana. Her eyes grew heavy and she succumbed to a warm peace spreading through her body. Alder was protecting her against the vale's defenses. Every day the vale's walls were thickening, which meant reentering the realm would be painful, like a million pins pricking her skin.

Her eyes fluttered open as they walked through a rippling wall of magic, entering the fae realm. They crossed a footbridge, headed for the place she most dreaded. "The queen," she muttered as her ice castle appeared on top of the mountain.

"Shh." Alder brushed his hand down her face. "Sleep. You are safe."

15

MASIE RUSHED into the bedchamber that she shared with Adaira. "Wake up," she exclaimed, "Leana is gone."

Her sister stirred slowly. "Leana is gone?"

"Aye. I've searched the whole keep I can no' find her. We can no' lose her again."

Adaira sat up. "She has no' run away, Masie. She's saving us by surrendering to the queen."

"How do ye know?"

"Because she ran away to protect us before. This time, I'm afraid she's no' coming back."

Masie sat on the edge on the bed and hung her head. "We can no' allow her to sacrifice her life for ours. We all took the blood oath."

"I know, Masie. Her guilt weighs too heavily on her heart."

"So, are we going to let her go?"

"Damn the devil, no." Adaira threw the furs back and got out of bed. "We stand together."

Masie joined her sister, helping her dress. "I'm no' afraid. I'm ready to send the queen back to hell."

"Me too. Before we leave, I need to talk with Kendrick. If we have any chance of saving Leana, we'll need his help."

"Aye, love conquers all."

"Aye, sister."

"I dinnae understand why ye will no' help us," Masie exclaimed. "Ye do love her?"

Kendrick sat at the table with his arms folded. His jaw ticked with anger as he listened to Masie's plea. Leana was no longer his concern, nor were her sisters. "Leana has made her bed, she can lie in it."

Adaira leaned across the table. "She has gone back to the fae queen in order to save us all. Ye owe it to her to bring her home."

"I owe her nothing. She brought this evil to me family."

"Ye dinnae understand, the queen is far eviler than us. I can no' allow Leana to suffer for the rest of her life."

Kendrick froze. If the stories were true, the winter fae were as evil and cunning as the devil himself. Meddling in fae business was strongly discouraged by the Druids if you valued your life. The Unseelies and Druids had history. The Druids had lost the great war, the survivors enslaved. It wasn't until the spring and summer fae court when his people were set free.

Aye, he knew how powerful and evil the queen was. He wished Leana's fate could be changed, but he wasn't the man to bring her justice.

"I'm sorry, I can no' help ye. 'Tis time ye leave now." Kendrick walked to the door and opened it.

No more words were spoken as Adaira and Masie made their way out the door. Adaira walked past him and a chill of anger streamed down his spine. Masie followed behind, but stopped before she crossed the threshold. "Know this, everything Leana did was out of love. I pray ye find it in yer heart to forgive her before it's too late."

Kendrick dropped his gaze to the floor as he shut the door.

"Ye are a fool," Finn exclaimed from across the room.

"This is no matter of yers." Kendrick made his way back to the table and sat down with a sigh. He scrubbed his hands down his face.

"Kendrick, this is no' time to be hanging onto yer foolish pride. Go after her."

"Damn it, Finn. I listened to ye once and look where it has gotten me. I will no' go after her. I can no' risk me family's safety."

Finn took a seat next to Kendrick. "Ye can no' deny that she has made ye a better person. She loves yer children as if they were her own. And God bless her, she must be a saint for putting up with yer stubborn arse."

Frustrated, Kendrick rested his elbows on the table. He hated it when Finn was right. He'd never quit loving Leana, no matter what she was. Hell, he hadn't been completely honest with her.

"Kendrick, I know ye to be an honorable man. Even when ye lost yer way, ye have always done the right thing. Do it now. Ye're the only one that can defeat the fae queen."

Kendrick looked up as realization washed over him.

"Ye know I'm right."

"Finn, ye're an arse," Kendrick huffed.

"Aye, the arse that's going to save yers." Finn grinned.

"Ready me horse." Kendrick stood. "I'll meet ye in the barn. There's something I need from the shop before I leave."

Finn nodded.

"And I'll need ye to watch over the children. I dinnae know when I'll be home."

"Aye." Finn quit the great hall.

In his heart, Kendrick knew he was doing the right thing. Without Leana, his world had spun out of control. She showed him how to love again.

"Damn the devil." Kendrick strode off to the shop and prepared for the battle of his life.

16

THE SMELL of rosewater startled Leana from sleep. She sat up in bed looking around the chamber as bits and pieces of familiarity flooded her mind. Things were much different here than back at the keep. Even though a bed, hearth, and wardrobe were in the bedchamber, it felt empty. Or mayhap, it was dread that filled the space.

Now that she was back at the queen's ice castle, all her hopes and dreams were gone. Her new life left her numb. After she made amends with queen, the real torture would begin. No one made a fool of her aunt without grave consequences. She wondered what her punishment would be. Nothing would take away the pain of losing Kendrick. She'd have eternity to suffer, and eternity wouldn't be long enough to forget him.

Leana got out of bed. The cold floor bit at her bare feet as she walked over to the wash basin. As she dried her face and hands, she noticed the sheer shift she was wearing. She ran her hands down her body. Her stomach lurched as she thought of Alder gazing at her naked body as he bathed her. She knew it was him who had dressed her and put her to bed. This was how it was going to be from now on. She'd be his pet.

"I see you're awake," A deep voice came from across the chamber and sent a chill down her spine.

Alder emerged from the shadows. She stumbled back as he approached. His long, black hair hung loosely past his shoulders. Black, scrolling tattoos peaked out from the neckline of his tunic. His ice-blue eyes were mesmerizing and matched his chilly demeanor.

"Aye, I've slept verra well. Do ye know when the queen will see me?"

Alder opened the wardrobe and pulled out a green, velvet dress with gold trim. "Come here, Leana."

Slowly, she padded across the chamber and stood in front of him. "When can I see the queen? She must know I'm here."

Why was he ignoring her? Alder gently pulled the dress the over her head. He walked to the corner of the room where he had been watching her and returned with a chair. He placed it in front of him. "Sit."

Leana did as he asked. There was no sense in arguing to see the queen. Her majesty would call for her when she was ready. Leana sat with her hands folded in her lap. She felt the prince pick up a handful of her hair and bring it to his nose. He inhaled deeply and sighed. "I've missed you."

Her stomach tightened. There wasn't one thing she missed about this place.

Alder gently ran a comb down her hair. "You've been a very busy traveler, haven't you?"

"We had to leave."

Alder yanked her hair back. His hot breath brushed against her skin. "You cannot outrun the queen, silly girl."

Leana grabbed his hand. "I have learned me lesson. I've come home to stay."

His grip loosened. "I have always loved you. I have given you freedom, and now you have fallen in love with a human. You dared to break the blood oath, which cannot go unpunished. I can forgive you, but I will not be able to protect you from the queen."

"Alder, I never knew how ye felt for me. Ye were like a brother."

Alder winced. "A brother?"

"Aye. I had to protect me family."

"No." He threw the comb across the chamber, then strode to the hearth. He gazed at the ceiling as he breathed in a calming breath. "I saw you with those two men in the blacksmith shop. It was me that killed them."

"Laird Cormag hunted us like a pack of wild dogs. Ye put me sisters in danger. What were ye thinking?"

"What was I thinking?" The flickering flames from the hearth cast a sinister glow on his face. "I wanted you to suffer like I had. I wanted you to feel the pain of your heart being ripped in two. I thought you'd come home after your clan banished you. I never thought you'd run away." Alder turned away as if he was ashamed at what he'd done. "I never meant to hurt you."

If Alder was capable of murder, what had he done to Kendrick? "What do ye mean?"

"Leana, you cannot lie to me. I've seen it with my own eyes. Heard it with my own ears. I was hiding in the kitchen when you confessed your love to that human. Aye, I was angry, but I didn't hurt him. This time, I wanted *you* to pay. When you summoned me, I was here telling the queen what I had seen and that I had found you."

"What?" Leana couldn't believe what she was hearing. "You would betray me like this?"

"I have ignored the queen's orders far too long. It was time I brought her the ultimate prize."

"Prize?"

"Leana, I cannot control myself around you. I adore you, and then you turn around and do something stupid. And trust me, woman, you will be punished."

Leana hung her head. "Please tell me ye will no' hurt Kendrick."

Alder returned to her side and took her hands in his. "No harm shall befall him as long as you stay in the realm. You can never see him again. Is that clear?"

Tears streamed down her checks. She couldn't speak but nodded.

"In time, you will forgive me and come to understand that everything I did was out of love. You know you can never change who you are, Leana. The more you try, the more people are hurt. 'Tis time you accept your Unseelie side."

Leana knew exactly what she was coming home to do, and it wasn't to be his pet. He was terribly mistaken, she'd never forgive him for the wicked things he'd done. And she would never embrace her Unseelie side.

Leana pulled her hands away. "I want to see Queen Snowdrop now."

"She's waiting for you in her solar."

Desperate to get the meeting over with, Leana went to the door. As soon as she touched the latch, her hand burned. Icy blue bars lined the walls. She was trapped inside her bedchamber by the queen's magic. She turned to the prince. "Alder, let me out."

"The queen is deeply hurt by your betrayal." He cupped her face. "I cannot protect you."

"I have never asked for your protection, nor do I want it. Now open the door."

With a flick of his wrist and a heavy sigh, Alder opened the door.

Leana rushed out and down the corridor to a winding staircase. It wrapped around five times before it touched the main hall. With haste, she made it to the queen's door. It had been a long time since she'd been inside the queen's solar. Nothing good ever happened there. But that was going to change now.

The air around her grew colder and smelled of blood. Fear unleashed inside Leana, but she must face the queen— for her sisters and for Kendrick and his children.

She sucked in a breath and knocked on the door. A young woman, pale as winter snow and wearing a long-sleeve robe, opened the door. Leana entered the chamber. The maid had puncture holes in her neck which made Leana think the queen would make her return to her old ways, hunting humans and bringing them back for Snowdrop to feed on. *Maiden, Mother, Crone.* What did her future hold?

Leana made her way through another long corridor. With each step, the ice floor creaked and echoed. She could barely hear her own thoughts over the pounding of her heart.

"Be brave, Leana," a familiar voice whispered.

"Mum?" She turned around, but no one was there.

Hearing her mother's voice could be a trick. The fae were unusually cruel and fed on anyone's fears and regrets. Leana continued down the corridor blocking out her mother's voice. Soon everything would be righted, and her family would be safe.

The corridor opened up to a huge chamber with ice walls. Five wide steps opened to the queen's bathing pool. Blood trickled down the stairs like a waterfall.

As Leana started to climb, Aspen stopped her. "The queen is bathing. Wait here."

The queen stood, blood trickling down her pale body. The sinister glare the queen gave Leana would have made the devil shudder. A slave dried the queen, then another wrapped her in a dark robe. As Snowdrop descended the steps, she pulled a pin from her hair.

Leana wasn't blinded as others would be by the queen's grace. Leana knew her bite was deadly, her soul as twisted as the rowan tree that bent around her throne.

Aye, Leana was going to pay dearly.

The queen smiled at Leana, but she didn't move, didn't even bow.

"You are in the queen's company. Kneel." Aspen pushed Leana to the floor. "Have you forgotten your place?"

She fell to her hands and knees.

Pain shot through Leana's hand as the prince stepped on it, grinding her fingers into the ice. "Address the queen properly," Aspen growled through clenched teeth.

"My Majesty."

The queen turned her head as if she didn't hear. Aspen kicked her in the ribs, knocking Leana to her side, and she heaved for air.

"The queen did not hear you," Aspen said.

Leana looked up at Aspen, and he grinned, revealing what pleasure he took in hurting her. With a stagger, Leana rose to her knees.

Show no weakness.

She bowed her head. "My Majesty."

Form the corner of her eye, Leana saw Alder enter the chamber and join his brother, Ash, in the back of the room. Leana didn't know why, but she looked to him for help. She needed someone on her side, for the queen would never understand why she'd betrayed her.

The queen stepped around her, hatred shining in her eyes. "You've finally came home, child," the queen said. She nodded to Asher and Alder and they left the chamber.

Seconds later, they returned with three women with hoods over their heads.

Leana didn't know what was happening. Her chest tightened as she thought about what the queen would have her do to repledge her loyalty. Would she have to kill three innocents to prove herself?

The princes brought the prisoners to the queen. "The blood oath can never be broken. No matter how far you run, you'll always belong to me." With a wave of her hand, the princes removed the women's hoods.

"Nay!" Leana charged forward, toward her sisters and mother, but Aspen held her back. "Nay!" Leana's knees buckled. "Please let them go."

"Go?" the queen spat. "You all have betrayed me, taken my lover, and plotted to kill me." She glared at Adaira. "Did you actually think you could take my kingdom with that pathetic army? Wolves are no threat to me, as for humans..." She snickered. "Pathetic. Now you want me to show you mercy?"

"Please," Leana begged.

The queen's lips curled down into a sneer. She grabbed Leana's chin, digging her nails into her skin. She leaned in close. "Why should I show you mercy?"

Leana stood steady. She knew how to save her family. "I've come to make you an offer."

"You and your sisters already belong to me. What could you possibly offer me?"

"My unwavering devotion."

Intrigued, the queen paused. "Go on."

"Me sisters never wanted to make the blood oath. They did it for me. I want you to release them. Release me mother from the troubles of the past. In return, I will serve ye and the realm forever."

The queen shook her head.

Leana had to think of something to convince the queen before she dismissed her. "You know it will only be a matter of time before we escape again. We did it once, we'll do it again. If ye let Masie and Adaira go, I'll swear allegiance to ye."

"Leana, I cannot let them go without something in return. A life for a life. You know the rules."

"Ye have mine."

"I need more. Fresh blood. You're asking to free three people in exchange for one."

"May I speak freely?" Leana asked.

The queen nodded.

"I'm asking ye to save yer family. Let them go, mend the past. Doughall isn't worth ruining yer relationship with yer sister."

The queen gazed at her sister, Helen. "I'm not interested in mending the past. What she did to me is unforgiveable. Laird Keith was mine."

"Laird Keith kidnapped our mother from Laird Gunn," Masie revealed. "'Tis true. I saw the tapestry."

"Masie." Helen held up her hand. "'Tis no' matter. Yer aunt knows and she still blames me."

"Enough," the queen commanded. "I do not care. 'Tis you that wants something from me. I suggest you tread softly. My patience is wearing thin."

"What do ye want me to do?" Leana asked.

"You ask me to free your mother and sisters and I get you in return. A life for a life, Leana." The queen paced, tapping her long, icy finger on her chin. "I need an heir to the throne."

Leana's heart dropped as she knew what the queen was thinking. An heir only meant one thing...an arranged marriage.

"I cannot have children of my own. By the oath, Leana, you are my daughter." The queen stopped and faced her. "I will release Adaira and Masie. Your mother is of no use to me. She's free to go. But you will wed Alder and give me an heir and many grandchildren."

"Will ye free Clan Keith and the Honor Guard from the dungeons?"

Frustrated, the queen threw her arms in the air. "Maiden, Mother, Crone! I'll free them all."

"Leana, ye can no' do this." Helen yanked free from the prince. She cupped Leana's face. "Me sweet, red-haired wildflower. Ye dinnae have to do this."

Leana leaned into her mother's gentle touch. By the gods, she wished she could go back in time. She wanted to be the little girl dancing with her sisters and mother in the summer sun. She wanted to be a girl without a care in the world.

Leana gazed into her mother's eyes. They were blue like hers. She'd never forgotten how they twinkled when she laughed. Her mother would laugh again. "Mother, I have to do this. 'Tis the only way for Adaira, Masie, and ye to be free from the queen. I started this nightmare and I will end it."

"Ye are as stubborn as me." Helen smiled, then turned to the queen. "I'm no' leaving here without me daughter."

"Mum, please."

Helen waved her hand. "Galanthus, ye're forgetting an important detail. A union between Alder and Leana will bind our house as allies. Their child will be as much mine as yers. Leana will be named a princess of the Unseelie court, and as her mother, I will stay here and be treated with respect."

Leana could see the hatred brewing in the queen's eyes. She'd been outwitted. "I suppose you are right, Helen. The wedding will happen tomorrow."

"Tomorrow?" Leana gasped.

"Yes, child. I want that grandchild soon," the queen said. "Now, if we're done, I have some business to attend to." She left the solar.

Adaira and Masie ran to their sister. "Leana, we'll think of a way out of this," Adaira promised.

"Aye, ye will no' marry that beast," Masie said as she hugged her. They wrapped their arms around each other and huddled together. "I have me girls back," Helen said through tears of joy. "As long as we have one another, we'll find a way out of this."

Leana broke away. "Nay, Mum. I will marry the prince. I will keep me word and there will be peace."

"What about Kendrick?" Adaira asked. "Ye love him."

Her heart fluttered when she heard his name. Happy memories of Anna, Allie, and Kit flashed before her eyes. She loved them with all her heart. Because of her, everyone she loved would be safe. "Aye, and this is why I must marry the prince."

Adaira shook her head. "Ye have a chance at happiness and ye're throwing it away like a fool."

"Adaira…" Helen scolded.

"Giving up on what makes ye happy is no' the answer. This place will poison yer heart. Over time, the queen will destroy the good in ye. Ye know what I say is the truth."

Leana did know, and it chilled her to the bone. How was she going to stay true to herself? Or did it really matter anymore? Without Kendrick, her life was empty. At least in the fae realm she wouldn't hurt anyone.

"I dinnae expect ye to understand, sister, but I must do this."

17

ADAIRA STRODE out of the queen's chamber and headed straight to the dungeon where Rafe and her men were being held. Inside, she raged like a tempest. She wouldn't allow Leana to follow through with her plan. All three sisters had taken the oath together and would be leaving the realm together.

Two guards barred her way, and she hissed, showing her fangs, daring them to make a move. She wouldn't think twice about ripping their heads off.

They parted, and she swung the door open, snatching a torch as she raced down the winding stairs. The stench of filth lingered in the air causing her stomach to sour. "Rafe," she called out.

"Aye."

She followed his voice to the back of the dungeon. "Wolf, I'm here."

The place was dark even with torchlight. Picking up the pace, she continued down the corridor praying that this wasn't fae trickery.

"Adaira!"

Startled, she turned around and bumped into a wall of muscle. "Rafe." She wrapped her arms around him. "Are ye hurt?" She took a step back and looked him over.

"No, my queen, I am not."

"How about yer men?"

"Well." Rafe cupped her face and kissed her deeply. "I was worried."

"I know. Me, too."

Rafe tipped her chin up. "What aren't ye telling me?"

"The queen is releasing all of us. Even Masie and I from the blood oath."

"That's incredible news." Rafe smiled.

Adaira wished she could feel joy, but she couldn't. It was far worse than she could imagine.

"Adaira." Rafe's smile faded. "What is it?"

Adaira shook her head. "Our freedom came at a high cost. Leana is to wed Alder, which will unite us with the queen."

"Shite." He blew out a frustrated breath.

"I know. But there's a way we can still beat the queen. Ye must find Kendrick and bring him here. He's the only one that can help Leana."

"I dinnae understand. How?"

"Rafe, the moment I met Kendrick, I knew there was something different about him. I could no' put me finger on it until now. He's a Druid."

"A Druid?"

"Aye, I felt his magic. He's the only one that can help us now. I can no' be tied to the queen any longer."

"My Queen, I'll do whatever ye ask of me."

"Bring Kendrick here by tomorrow."

"Tomorrow?"

"Aye."

Rafe shook his head. "Ye know this is impossible."

"No' for a wolf." She grinned.

"Lass, ye're lucky I love ye."

Adaira smiled as she watched Rafe gather his men and leave the dungeon. To make sure the queen kept her word, Adaira followed them out to the edge of the fae vale. As she watched Rafe leave her heart ached. She wouldn't rest easily until he returned with Kendrick.

"Godspeed, Wolf," she whispered.

———

Smoke billowed up ahead in the forest, alarming Kendrick. He slowed his horse. Through the night he'd tracked Leana's sisters through the glen in hope he'd find the fae mound. Had the queen found them before he had?

God's bones, he prayed he wasn't too late.

Kendrick dismounted at an abandoned campsite. His heart sank like rock when he eyed the destruction. The tents were tattered and burned, some still smoldering. Hoofprints were everywhere. Someone had attacked this camp. But where were the people?

Kendrick pulled his bow from behind his back, ready for whatever came his way. The place reeked of terror. Walking with an arrow at the ready, he continued to search the camp. Where were the bloody bodies?

Then he stopped. He couldn't see anything, but he heard footsteps. Shite, he had to find a place to hide.

Kendrick darted behind a tree. With his back against the trunk, he took in a deep breath, then peeked over his shoulder. Two men. Kendrick kept his eyes on them.

"He has to be here," the taller one said.

"Aye, he's here." The second tipped his chin at the tree where Kendrick was hiding.

Damn. Kendrick stepped into the open, his arrow aimed to kill. "Who are ye? What do ye want with me?"

The men held their hands up. "We mean no harm. Are ye Kendrick?"

"Aye, and if ye dinnae tell me why ye're here, I will kill ye."

"Adaira sent us to find ye. Leana is in trouble. She needs ye."

Kendrick lowered his bow. "Ye know where Leana is?"

"Aye." The taller of the two men approached him. "I'm Rafe, Adaira's husband. This here is my brother, Teg." Rafe held out his hand.

Kendrick eyed both men before he shook their hands. "Ye know Leana?"

"Aye," Rafe said.

"What happened here?" Kendrick asked.

"The queen's guard found us before Masie and Adaira returned from your home. We were all taken prisoner."

"What about Leana?"

"She's alive but needs you. The queen has arranged her to wed."

"Does she want this marriage?" Kendrick asked.

"No."

"Then we must stop it."

"Aye, we have no time to waste. The ceremony is tomorrow."

"Then let's make haste." Kendrick whistled and his horse came running.

"Follow us," Rafe said.

The two men shed their clothes, and their skin turned to

fur. They growled and snapped at the air as if they were going to rip Kendrick's throat out.

"What the devil?"

Before Kendrick knew what was happening, the wolves ran into the forest. Kendrick followed as the beasts weaved between trees and jumped over fallen logs and ice-covered streams. It was hard to keep up at times, but Kendrick had good reason to fight his way back to Leana—he must save her.

The air thickened as they went deeper into the forest, making it hard for Kendrick to breathe. Forced to slow down, he lost sight of the wolves.

"Rafe, Teg!"

He came upon a circle of six tall trees that looked to belong to the fae. He followed his instincts and entered the circle.

Once inside, the trees disappeared, and a grass-covered mound appeared. From behind the mound, he caught a glimpse of one of the wolves' tails.

"Wait." Kendrick gasped when he saw the wolf jump through a clear wall of ripples, then disappear.

He knew he had to go through the portal to reach the fae realm. He paused and stared at the wall, annoyed at himself for being scared. "It would be more inviting if ye had a door," he yelled out of frustration.

There had to be an easier way in. He didn't know what kind of magic sealed outsiders from going in. What if the fae knew he was coming and cursed the portal to kill Druids?

His Leana was in there somewhere and needed him.

Kendrick kicked his horse into a run, making a lap around the mound to gain speed. Entering the portal with speed was the only chance he had to protect his body from the power of destructive fae magic, though it wouldn't guarantee his safety.

The entrance was drawing near. He pushed faster, closed his eyes, then leapt into the fae realm. God help him.

18

LEANA STARED out into the great hall full of Unseelies. Their judgmental gazes would watch her every move, for she wasn't a true Unseelie. She was a Seelie turned.

Alder stood in black at the altar next to his brothers. Adaira and Masie waited on the other side. Leana couldn't stop shaking. She didn't want to be there and most definitely didn't want to marry the dark prince and become princess of the fae realm. She closed her eyes, but nothing could change this nightmare.

A vision hit her...

Her family gathered underneath a yew tree. A canopy of branches shaded them from the sun. Birds sang and danced from tree branch-to-tree branch welcoming a new season, a new beginning.

The guests parted and bowed as Leana walked down the pathway behind Anna and Allie who were sprinkling white rose petals on the ground. As she reached the end of the aisle, a man with long, gray-streaked hair smiled at her. Kendrick. She lost herself in his dark smoldering gaze. Nothing existed but Kendrick and her. This was the man she was destined to marry.

Music from the present reminded Leana of what she was about to do. Kendrick was a dream she'd forever keep with her.

"Leana, are ye ill?" Her mother was standing next to her.

Leana didn't want to open her eyes. She'd rather dream a wee bit longer. "I'm fine." She opened her eyes and smiled, but Helen saw through her it.

"Ye dinnae have to do this," Helen said. "We can find another way."

Hours ago, Helen had pleaded with her not to marry the prince. However, Leana had meddled with fate one too many times. In her dream, she'd seen her future, but it would never come true. This was her punishment, and a sacrifice she was willing to make in order to keep peace with the queen. She'd live in the fae realm to keep her family safe.

"Please, Leana, think twice about what yer giving up."

Every plea from her mother broke her resolve not to run, for that was what the old Leana would have done. She'd never outrun the queen. No more blood would be shed because of Leana.

"Mum, ye know I can no'. This is me home now. Promise to take Masie and Adaira home. I dinnae want ye to stay here. Ye deserve better."

"Leana, ye're me daughter. I can no' leave ye alone to suffer. We'll find a way to bring ye home."

"Mum…"

Asher looked around the corner, signaling it was time for them to walk down the aisle.

"Ye are a beautiful bride," Helen said.

Leana felt like a princess in her off-the-shoulder, blue grown. Two long, red braids framed her face and the rest of her hair had been gather in neat bun on the back of her head. The braids were wrapped in jeweled clips, and a band of snowdrop flowers and ivy sat upon her head. The queen had insisted she wear them.

She took in her mother's comforting smile.

"Leana, I'll always be with ye. I love ye."

Her heart tightened. Leana couldn't give in, she had to do this. "I love ye too, Mum."

One foot in front of the other. She reached the altar where Alder eagerly took her hand. Her mother's glare spoke louder than words; she wasn't handing her daughter over to him willingly.

"Mum, everyone is watching," Leana whispered. "Please."

Helen kissed her cheek, then took a seat.

Leana's knees threatened to buckle as she turned and faced Alder. He brought her hands to his mouth and kissed them. "I will make you very happy."

Leana forced a smile, then turned her attention to the queen who was standing in front of them.

"On behalf of the winter court and realm, I, Queen Snowdrop, welcome you to the wedding between Prince Alder and Leana Keith. The fact you all have traveled so far to join us, is a testament of your support and loyalty to the crown." The queen took both their hands. "Leana, Alder, a marriage not only unites the two of you, but brings the promise of new life. A new life the two of you will share. And from your union will spring new life that will ensure its people remain pure, strong, and powerful." The queen raised her arms to the audience. "Before I begin, is there anyone here that objects to this union?" The queen's icy glare blazed over her guests, daring the Unseelies to challenge her.

"I do."

Surprised, Leana whipped around to find Kendrick perched in the balcony with an arrow aimed at the queen. "I'm here to take back what's mine."

An arrow, glowing like a star, whizzed through the air and hit the queen in the chest. The queen clutched her breast and gasped. Black blood gushed from the wound.

"Druid," she hissed as she removed the arrow.

The hall grew eerily silent.

Then an army of horses arrived, shaking the hall.

Leana stared at Helen in disbelief. "Mother, what have ye done?"

A ray of light blasted through the arched entrances, blinding Leana as she tried to make sense of what was happening.

The bright light dimmed and what Leana saw next was breath taking. At least a hundred Seelie fae on white horses with their swords drawn were ready for battle.

"Sister," Helen confronted the queen. "I will only ask ye this once, stand down and leave peacefully. I dinnae want to kill ye."

The queen burst into laughter. "The Seelie's are weak. Ye cannot best me." The queen motioned for her guards. "My men will have your heads."

Helen signaled to the commander of the cavalry. Another unit of Seelie soldiers charged into the hall with a pack of wolves, each soldier carrying a spear with an Unseelie head skewered on it. Leana cringed at the sight.

The queen snarled.

"Stand down," Helen commanded.

Ash and Aspen drew their swords and shielded the queen. "You will fight for your queen," Ash yelled out to the Unseelie guests.

The hall roared as the Unseelies gathered to protect their ruler.

"Leana!" Kendrick's voice rang out.

Looking through the throng of fae, wolves, and humans, she found Kendrick fighting his way to her. Her fear melted away. He was fighting for her. She looked at Alder as he protected his queen. If there was any chance of her making it out of here without him or the queen noticing, it was now. She grabbed a sword from a fallen Seelie and took off toward Kendrick, ducking arrows.

A body dropped next to her and bright red blood splattered on her face; a drop landed on her lips causing her to stop abruptly. She licked her lips. The blood was sweet and human. Her chest tightened and she burned for more. There was so much blood in the hall, she could feed for days.

A Clan Keith lad who had just slayed an Unseelie won her attention. His veins pumped fiercely. She narrowed in on him. He was healthy and strong. Her gums throbbed as she imagined his warm, thick blood rolling over her tongue.

"Nay," Leana shook her head, fighting the *Baobhan sith* urge to sink her fangs into the lad's flesh, but it was too strong. The battle between her human side and blood drinker side raged inside her. She held on to what little resolve she had left. She wouldn't kill the lad.

"Control it, Leana." She took a deep breath.

"Leana!"

She heard Kendrick's voice but couldn't see him. Her blood hunger had left her in a daze.

"Lass." He cupped her face. "Can ye hear me?"

Slowly, she recovered.

"Are ye well?"

She began to answer him then realized her fangs were

out. She shook her head, and he wrapped his arms around her. She melted against him.

"I'm going to get ye out of here."

"Ye're no' safe." Leana stepped from his embrace. A snarl escaped her mouth revealing her fangs.

Kendrick cupped her face. "Look at me, lass. This is no' who ye are. Fight it."

She shook her head and averted her gaze. She couldn't "Please, Kendrick, I dinnae want to hurt ye."

"I didnae come all this way for naught. Look at me." He held her firmly, making her look at him. "I love ye, lass. *All of ye.*"

The ice surrounding her heart melted at his confession. He loved her, even the beastly side. He was risking everything for her. She blinked, recovering control of her senses. Reaching up, she caressed his stubbled jaw and lost herself within the depths of his dark eyes. He was her destiny. He was home.

With each breath the beast faded away. "Ye shot the queen," she said in disbelief.

Kendrick smiled. "Me aim is always true and me arrows deadly."

"I always knew there was something different about ye, Druid."

He dipped his head and claimed her lips. Tingles raced down her body, straight to her toes.

"Leana," he murmured against her lips. "We need to get out of here."

Numbness spread throughout her body and she went limp. What was happening? This was more than a kiss. She couldn't move. A sharp pain nipped her back as if she'd been stung by a bee. A tidal wave of pain crashed through her. *Maiden, Mother, Crone!*

She clutched her chest and felt something sharp—metal. She looked down at her blood-soaked hand. She'd been struck with an arrow.

She looked up at Kendrick. He was screaming. Nay, this couldn't be happening. She couldn't be dying. She fought to keep her eyes open, for if they shut, she feared they'd close forever.

Darkness claimed her as she fell against Kendrick. *I love ye, lass* were the last words she heard.

19

"NAY!" Kendrick yelled as he grabbed the arrow sticking from Leana's back. He broke the shaft off. "Shite!"

He stared at the glowing shaft. One of his poison arrows had struck her. He fell to his knees, holding her in his arms. "Wake up, lass!" He pushed her hair from her face. Her veins glowed with poison. If he didn't remove the arrowhead quickly, Leana would die.

"Her love for you was strong. I never had a chance to feel it." Alder said as he stood in front of Kendrick, lowering the bow in his hand.

Kendrick gently laid Leana on the ground and stood. He fisted his hands as rage unleashed inside him. "Ye did this?"

"I had no choice. I'm through cleaning up her messes."

Kendrick couldn't believe what he was hearing. "She left ye no choice? I dinnae understand."

"Leana could never be human. She'd never let the dream of being your wife and the mother of your children go."

"She shouldn't have to. I want her in me life, need her like the air I breathe."

"We both want what we cannot have, Druid."

With lightning speed, Kendrick drew an arrow from his quiver, notched it, and aimed at the prince's heart. "Leana will be avenged." He released the arrow.

The prince dropped to his knees. "Killing me will not bring her back."

"Aye. But killing ye will make me feel much better." Kendrick launched arrow after arrow into the prince. The bastard would die for what he'd done. Kendrick continued firing until the prince fell to the ground.

Then he retrieved the arrows for reuse. "Kill them all," he roared, firing into the crowd, needing to satisfy his growing rage.

When the last Unseelie begged for his worthless life, Kendrick had an arrow for him, too.

He lowered his bow, exhausted from the fight. "Leana," he exclaimed and ran over to her. He abruptly stopped as Masie and Adaira held their sister.

"What happened?" Masie asked. "She's immortal. An arrow can no' wound her."

Kendrick shoved his hand through his hair. "We must remove the arrow. 'Tis poisonous. She'll die if we dinnae."

Kendrick unsheathed a dagger from his boot. "'Tis will no' be pretty, lass."

"I dinnae care about pretty. Save her," Adaira cried.

"Masie, roll Leana onto her stomach. I need to see how deep the arrow is lodged."

Masie nodded, and with help from her mother, they turned Leana over. Kendrick ripped the back of her wedding dress open. He paused when someone tapped his shoulder.

"Here." Kerr handed him a skin. "'Tis whiskey."

Kendrick poured the whiskey over the wound. He knew

right where to cut and readied the dagger. He looked up at Masie. "Hold onto her, lass."

"Aye."

Leana winced as he cut into her flesh.

"I'm sorry, lass," Kendrick said. "It will be over soon."

He slid his finger inside the incision, following the shaft to the arrowhead. The tip wasn't bent, so extracting it would be easier than he first thought. Holding his breath, he eased it out.

He poured the rest of the whiskey over the wound, then yanked his tunic off, soaking up the blood. "We need bandages."

Adaira and Helen tore strips from their gowns.

"This should help." Adaira said.

"Masie, can ye sit Leana up?"

"Aye." With Kerr's help, she repositioned her sister.

Kendrick wrapped the strips around her chest, covering the wound. When he was done, he took her into his arms. Her skin was paler than before. Her breathing was steady, but slow. He needed the remedy to the poison.

"Let's get her in bed, Kendrick," Helen said. "What else can we do?"

As much as he wanted to take Leana home, he knew in her condition she'd never make it. He scooped Leana in his arms and stood.

"I'll take ye to her bedchamber," Masie said.

"Thank you. I will also need some *salan lus*, self-heal."

"I will see what I can find," Adaira said.

Kendrick followed Masie out of the hall and down a corridor. Everything carved in ice began to melt and facture. By the time they reached the end of the hallway, Kendrick noticed something peeking out from the crack in the floor. "Masie, what's going on. Are we safe?"

"Aye. The ice is melting. Winter died when the Unseelie were defeated. Spring is here, along with a new court of Seelies. I've never witnessed the change before. Everything is new and beautiful." Masie looked upset.

"What's wrong?"

"'Tis beautiful for a Seelie. But for an Unseelie, the sun can be dangerous."

"What do ye mean?"

"When we came of age, the queen made us drink human blood. The more we drank, the more Unseelie we became. Our mother hid that we had been born Seelies. Growing up we believed we were human. We lived a human life. 'Tis my opinion if Leana knew we were Seelies she'd never have made the blood oath with the queen."

"So, ye can no' enjoy the wonders that spring brings?"

"Aye. We must forever live in darkness."

Kendrick looked down at Leana as they climbed a winding staircase. *Forever in darkness?* Once back at home, he'd have a lot of changes to make to accommodate Leana. He'd do whatever it took to make her happy. She'd never truly live in darkness.

He couldn't lose her again, it would destroy him.

They finally reached the bedchamber, and Kendrick placed Leana on the bed.

"I'll fetch water and clean bandages," Masie said.

Kendrick nodded, he couldn't look away from Leana. "I love her, Masie."

Masie walked behind him and put her hand on his shoulder. "I know."

"She's me everything."

"I have all the faith in ye, Kendrick, that ye will save her. She'll come back to ye."

Masie left the chamber, and Adaira joined him.

"I found a jar of self-heal and some whiskey. I even brought two cups," she jested.

Kendrick grinned. "I suppose ye're no' leaving any time soon."

"No' a chance, Druid. I want to be here and see ye work yer magic on me sister." She filled the tankards halfway. "'Tis going to be a long night."

Kendrick removed the rest of Leana's tattered dress and soiled bandages. He cleaned the wound with whiskey, then applied the self-heal as Adaira ripped a sheet into strips. They wrapped her wound, then he tucked her into bed.

He brushed her hair away from her face. She was burning up and there was nothing more he could do except pray that the remedy would work. Grief stricken, Kendrick fell to his knees, angry at himself for not protecting her, angry at the bastard who dared to take her from him, angry that this might be their last night together. He held her hand. "Aye, 'tis going to be a long a night."

20

SOMETHING PULLED Leana from her deep sleep. She opened her eyes, gazing about the room. Candles were lit, glowing like a warm summer day. Vibrant bluebells surrounded her. They were scattered on the mantel, on her bedside table, and on the bed. Where was she?

Slowly, she sat up. Pain ripped through her and she clutched her chest. She pulled back the covers. "Maiden, Mother, Crone." She winced as she took in the blood-soaked bandage wrapped around her chest. *What happened to me?* Panic set in. Someone had hurt her. But who? She closed her eyes, struggling to remember, but her mind was foggy. *Think, Leana, think.*

Confused and terrified of what was waiting for her, she threw the rest of the covers off. *What the devil?* She was naked. She stood and wrapped a fur about her. But her legs were too weak and she sank to the floor. "Nay," she exclaimed. "I have to move."

The chamber door opened. Bright light spilled inside and she shielded her eyes. "Please, go away." She scooted to a dark corner, fighting to see again.

Footsteps sounded, and she struggled to see who it was.

"Leana!" Adaira cried.

Relief washed over Leana—she was safe. "Aye."

"Ye're awake." Adaira pulled her into a suffocating hug. "I thought we lost ye."

"If ye dinnae stop squeezing me, ye'll kill me."

"Sorry." Leana felt her sister's icy touch as she brushed her hair from her face. "Ye are safe here."

Finally, her sister's smiling face came into focus. "'Tis really ye."

"Aye, let's get ye back in bed." Adaira lifted her to her feet.

Leana's toes tingled and a warm sensation ran up her legs. "What happened to me? Where are we?"

"Leana, do ye remember the wedding?"

She paused, recalling walking down the aisle to the dark prince. "Aye." Her eyes grew large. "Did I—"

"Nay. By the mercy of the gods, ye didnae wed. Kendrick and I made sure of it."

A flash of an arrow flying through the air and hitting the queen flickered in her mind. "Aye, Kendrick shot the queen."

"On me order, Rafe and Teg found Kendrick and brought him here."

"Is he here?" Leana was desperate to be reunited with him.

Adaira nodded.

Leana's legs gave out again, but Adaira caught her. "Ye should be in bed. Ye're still fighting the poison."

"Poison?"

"Do ye remember the fae battle?"

The sound of steel on steel ricocheted through her head as she pieced together the chaos. "I was fighting me way to

Kendrick when suddenly the hall went dark. I remember nothing after that."

"Leana, this is no' easy for me to say."

"Tell me."

"Alder tried to kill ye with one of Kendrick's poison arrows."

Leana sat on the edge of the bed in disbelief. Alder tried to kill her? She couldn't believe it. As a child, Alder was always there for her, watching over her, protecting her like a brother. However, she'd sensed a darkness inside him that at times chilled her to the bone. "Is he—"

"Dead? Aye, ye have been avenged."

She covered her mouth. "Kendrick?"

"He loves ye unconditionally."

"Leana!" Masie rushed in. "Ye're awake!" She squealed and ran to Leana, throwing her arms around her.

"Aye, Masie."

"How do ye feel?"

"Like I've been shot with an arrow."

They giggled.

"I knew Kendrick would save ye," Masie beamed.

"What do ye mean?" Leana asked. Had Kendrick been in her bedchamber? Where was he?

"He's been tending to yer wound and giving ye the remedy for the poison."

"Me beautiful daughter." Leana's heart dropped to her stomach as her mother entered the room. She hugged her mom and held on tight, for if this was all a dream she didn't want to wake.

"Mum, I'm sorry for everything. Please forgive me."

"Sweet lass, no need to apologize. I know yer heart."

Her mother's touch broke her down. Tears streamed

down her face as the guilt bled out of her. "I never meant to hurt anyone," Leana sobbed.

All of the women hugged Leana at the same time. "We stand together."

"Aye," Masie sniffled. "Together."

Helen cupped her face. "Lass, thank ye for being brave." She looked at Adaira and Masie. "All of ye are. Now, let's put this part of our lives behind us. The winter Unseelie court has been defeated, and the Seelie spring court now rules over the fae. Winter is dead. The sun will shine on us again."

"Mum," Adaira said. "The sun will never shine on us."

"Ye are mistaken, me sweet." Helen retrieved three, scarlet pouches from her belt. She gave one to each sister.

Leana opened it and pulled out an amber amulet attached to a delicate chain. She held it in the palm of her hand, rubbing the top with her thumb as she admired its craftsmanship. "'Tis beautiful." Gold and silver flecks swirled inside the amulet. She looked at her mother. "What is this?"

"My loves, this amulet holds a special power. 'Tis no' verra often that the Seelie healer will produce such an artifact. This amulet gives ye the power to withstand the sun. As long as ye wear it, ye'll never have to fear the light." Helen took the necklace from Leana and placed it around her neck.

Adaira and Masie put theirs on too.

"Wear them wisely," Helen cautioned, "for there is no replacing them."

As soon as Leana could walk again, she knew exactly where she'd go—her mother's garden at Dornoch Castle. Even now, she could smell the fragrant flowers and remembered the endless joy she felt being there with her family.

Someone cleared their throat in the doorway. Leana looked up—Kendrick! Their gazes locked, and she melted.

Helen and her sisters left the bedchamber, giving Leana the privacy she and Kendrick needed.

———

Kendrick held back his excitement. He wanted to take Leana in his arms and never let her go but seeing her like this…it drove the dagger farther into his bleeding heart. He'd failed to protect her.

He walked over and grabbed some bandages and the jar of self-heal, then returned to Leana's bedside. "I see ye're awake."

Leana nodded.

He sat down on the bed fidgeting with bandages. He averted his gaze but could feel her eyes on him. He cleared his throat. "Ye've been asleep for a fortnight."

"I needed me beauty rest," Leana jested.

Leana's giggle slammed into his chest. He held onto his resolve pushing back the urge to break down right in front of her.

"Kendrick, why won't ye look at me?" Leana asked.

Kendrick had failed to protect the woman he loved. The shame he felt… He finally gazed at her. The blood on her bandage made him frown. "I should change that." He reached over, but before he could touch her, Leana took his hand in hers. "Talk to me, Kendrick."

Confessing his feelings was something he was never good at. The past two weeks had worn him down. He'd been prepared to lose her to the poison. Old wounds of losing his wife had reopened; wounds he didn't want to relive. But one thing never wavered…he loved this woman wholeheartedly.

"I'm sorry, lass."

"For what?"

Kendrick pointed to the wound.

"This?" Leana patted her chest. "Ye didnae do this to me."

"I failed to protect ye."

"If ye hadn't made those arrows, the queen would still be alive." She caressed his cheek, lifting his chin so he had to look at her. "Ye saved me. Kept me from marrying an evil man. Our children would have been wee beasties. I want to have babies with ye."

"I dinnae know what I would've become if I lost ye." Tears burned his eyes. "By the gods, lass, I need ye like the air I breathe." He shoved his hands in her hair, remembering the soft tendrils.

"I'm here, Kendrick," she whispered against his lips. "We have nothing to fear. I'm yers, body and soul."

He claimed her lips passionately. It seemed like forever since he'd tasted her kiss, felt the softness of her body. He rested his forehead against hers. "Ye've bewitched me, lass. I'd do anything to keep ye."

"Ye killed an evil fae queen. That's impressive."

"Aye." He chuckled.

"There is one thing ye haven't given me yet." Leana twirled a lock of his hair between her fingers.

"What might that be?"

"A baby girl," she grinned.

"A wee one," Kendrick coughed, not expecting such a request. However, the thought of adding a bairn to their family made him giddy.

"Well..."

"Of course. Once ye're well—" Kendrick paused as he watched Leana shake her head.

"Ye want to start...now?" Kendrick stuttered.

Leana nodded, smiling so much it hurt. "I dinnae want to waste any more time. Tomorrow, I want to go home. I miss the girls and Kit. And maybe even Finn."

"There's nothing I want more." He cupped her face, kissing her deeply as he laid her down. It was the first night of their future together, their forever.

EPILOGUE

Dornoch Castle, one year later...

Leana sat underneath a yew tree just outside her mother's garden. Children's laughter, squeaks, and screeches filled her ears as she watched her nieces and Allie frolic through the garden.

Leana's vision for her future had come true. Surrounded by family, she'd married Kendrick right under the yew ten months ago. It was the happiest time of her life, until now.

Leana gazed lovingly at her infant daughter suckling at her breast. She rubbed her red, fuzzy head and smiled. Kendrick had made her the happiest woman alive.

Aye, life with Kendrick was good. His dependency on ale was no longer an issue, which made his relationship with Anna stronger. He'd even given Anna and MacTavish his blessing to wed.

"Did ye see it?" Masie asked excitedly, disrupting Leana's daydream.

Leana watched her sister chase a waddling, blond-headed boy. "Duncan's first steps."

"Och!" Leana exclaimed as Duncan lost his balance and fell on his butt.

"Oh, me sweet laddie." Masie ran to her son and picked him up. "Yer papa will be so proud of ye." She joined Leana under the tree.

"Such a smart lad," Leana wiped a tear from her nephew's face.

"Kerr will be upset that he missed Duncan's first steps." Masie sat down.

"Aye, I hope the hunt is successful," Leana said. "With the lassies outnumbering the men in our house, Kendrick and Kit needed to get out and do something manly."

Masie giggled. "If I allowed it, Kerr would have taken Duncan with him. He can no' wait to take him hunting and to teach him to wield a sword." The excitement left Masie's voice.

"Masie, What's wrong?"

"As much as I want to believe in our happy life, I know there's a part of me that grows inside him. I can no' ignore the darkness."

Adaira joined them with her two babes, one on each hip. "I need a wet nurse," she huffed as she placed the babes on a blanket next to Leana. "Two mouths to feed...I can no' keep up."

Leana and Masie smiled.

"At least ye have one of each," Masie said.

"Aye." Adaira smiled down at her son and daughter. "The wee beasties look just like their father."

Leana loved seeing this side of Adaira. The twins had softened her rough edges. "I think Seren looks like ye." Leana saw a shadow of grief pass over Adaira's face. "Ye have no heard from Rafe's sister?"

"Nay, Seren hasn't come home."

"Och, ye honor her well by naming yer first born after her."

"Aye," Adaira smiled. "I still have no' given up hope. Seren will come home one day." Adaira glanced at Masie, noticing her frown. "This is a joyous day, aye?"

"Masie's scared,"

"I'm no' scared," Masie denied. "I'm concerned."

"About what?" Adaira asked.

"Our children. Ye can no' ignore who we are. We have taken great risks in having babes. Ina saw the darkness in Duncan. Our children are not like the others."

"Masie, do no' fash. We are here to teach them the ways of our life," Leana said.

"Aye, we overcame the darkness, so our bairns will no' have to,' Adaira added.

Leana understood Masie's concerns, for she couldn't deny it, the same thoughts had plagued her mind. Staring down at her daughter, Leana would move heaven and earth to protect her. "We have always stood together. We can conquer anything that comes our way."

"Ye're right, sister," Masie said, smiling. "Together, we can do anything."

"Aye," Adaira agreed. "We suffered too long. 'Tis our time to be happy."

The queen was dead, the winter court had been defeated, and Kendrick was by her side. Indeed, it was her time to be happy.

"By the way, Leana," Adaira said. "Ye daughter is a month old and the poor child hasn't a name. Have Kendrick and ye picked one out yet?"

"Aye, her name is Davina."

About Victoria Zak

Victoria Zak is an internationally bestselling author of historical and contemporary romance. She weaves magic into her timeless tales, reminding readers anything is possible, especially with a dragon by your side. Raised in Dunedin, Florida, the sister city to Stirling, Scotland, no wonder she grew up fascinated with anything Scottish. Add the ocean into the mix, and it's easy to see where Victoria found inspiration for her stories.

As a child, she read anything she could get her hands on, which developed into full-scale book addiction by adulthood. Curious by nature, Victoria doesn't shy away from anything. She enjoys historical research and people watching is her favorite sport. Victoria currently resides in Maryland with her real-life heroes, her husband and two children.

Victoria loves to hear from her readers. You can connect with her through the links below:

www.victoriazakromance.com
victoria@victoriazakromance.com

MORE BOOKS BY VICTORIA ZAK

Guardians of Scotland Series:

Highland Burn

Highland Storm

Highland Fate

Highland Destiny

Daughters of Highland Darkness Series:

Beautiful Darkness

Deadly Darkness

Wicked Darkness

Hell's Cowboys Series:

My Immortal Cowboy

Stand Alones:

De Wolfe's Honor

Once Upon a Winter Solstice

The Jewel of Grim Fortress

Midnight's Kiss

www.ingramcontent.com/pod-product-compliance
Lightning Source LLC
Chambersburg PA
CBHW051946170626
46808CB00007B/2509